Submerged Ever After

"Light a candle and see my face in the mirror of your soul, not within an earthly mirror."

Ann Marie Ruby

Disclaimer:

This book ("***SUBMERGED EVER AFTER***") in no way represents or endorses any religious, philosophical, political, or scientific view. It has been written in good faith for people of all cultures and beliefs. This book has been written in American English. There may be minor variations in spelling due to translations.

This is a work of fiction. Names, characters, places, and incidents are the product of the author's imagination or are used fictitiously. Any resemblance to actual persons, living or dead, is purely coincidental. References to historical events, real people, or real locations are used fictitiously.

Published in the United States of America, 2026.

ISBN-13: 979-8-9950595-0-9

Dedication

What is love? Is it a face you see in front of you? Or is it an imprint left on your soul throughout eternity? This immortal love story I dedicate to all twin flames separated by the ocean of life and death, not through time or distance but through a heartbeat.

N
W
E
S
Dead Queen's Island

Table Of Contents

Prologue:

The Dead Queen's Castle

"Haunted
castle by the ocean,
all fear as the
residents have
been dead for a
thousand
years. Why is it
that you fear not
the living, but the
Dead Queen's
Castle?"

The Indian Ocean meets the Pacific Ocean at the South East Cape of Tasmania, Australia. At that magical spot is a hidden piece of paradise called the Dead Queen's Island. Although the island was discovered a long, long time ago, it is not known to many people. To this day, it has been mostly left alone. Some call it a phantom island because the island at times disappears, and one wonders was it there or was it a temporary mirage. Some locals even compare it to a ghost island because they say the island appears to the world every few hundred years.

It's like a fog appears and covers the whole island to give it privacy, so no one can find it. You can enter or exit only by boat. No roads or bridges connect this piece of land to the rest of the world. Residents of this island can take a boat out to the main island of Tasmania to see any kind of real civilization. If anyone wants some peace and quiet, the Dead Queen's Island is the perfect place to get it.

Although there are inhabitants, a large part of the island is left deserted. It is rumored indigenous people who like to be left alone are given their privacy there, but they too appear and disappear every few hundred years. The mysterious island is getting a lot of attention nowadays as more people are finding out about it.

A romantic tragedy about parting lovers made headlines with the tourists. Legend has it that an emotionally agonized woman's painful cries rip through the island. Everyone curses the man who mysteriously disappeared, leaving her behind. It would be a nice story to write a novel about, but I like happy endings. For some reason, tragedies, even fictional, churn a sensitive spot within my soul I don't want to walk into.

The spiritual feeling of longing hurts my inner soul. I do believe in rebirth, but I wonder if my dream girl had left me, or if I had left her. The painful thoughts of being separated from one another is not a story I particularly would write. My thought is we have so many tragedies, so with my pen, we can have a happily ever after. Who in their right mind wants to be Romeo? Not me.

The ship crew members were all busy talking amongst each other, yet they froze at the first sight of a majestical structure that became visible slowly and quietly. Something was very wrong about the place. There was a bone-chilling quietness amongst the crew. Suddenly, everyone on board the boat went back to talking and planning what they would do when they went back home. I assumed they were all free from the magnetic spell of the castle.

From far away, I saw an ancient structure, the castle, that I purchased was standing high above a hill on the small island. The castle that brought me to the island was built with ancient stones. The castle grounds were designed so no one could enter or leave easily as there were tall stone walls and a very old moat with a draw bridge that led to the castle gate. On top of the castle was a lighthouse with a huge two-story lantern room. The lantern must have guided the ships, the boats, and all people traveling to and from the castle. This larger-than-life sized beacon of light warned the islanders of all imminent threats.

I felt the whole property was looking at me, warning me of upcoming dangers I would face if I opened the castle doors. Fear gripped my soul as I wondered for the hundredth time if I should have avoided this castle. Yet the danger that I felt inside of my gut also attracted me even more to the castle. I was being pulled like a magnet. I knew somehow my life would change drastically if I entered the castle. My whole being was preparing itself for a dangerous battle which I couldn't predict but knew was looming ahead.

As my private cruise ship reached closer to the island, I was triggered by some kind of intense adrenaline. The effects were very unusual for me as I could sense the hair on my arms stand up. My whole body had goosebumps.

I had an eerie feeling like I was here before. I asked myself why did this place and everything my eyes were witnessing seem familiar. Was I here before? Without ever placing my feet on the island, I bought this property blindly. Even then, everything seemed so familiar, yet so unfamiliar at the same time.

I had the feeling like when I jump up and wake up from my sleep, I know I was seeing a dream, but I forget my dream. It's usually somewhere in my mind but it's like I can't pull the pictures out from the mind fog to put them together. Was it just my longing for the unsolved love story that was rumored and whispered about on this island? Maybe it was the stories my ship crew tried to put into my ears while I slept trying to avoid them. Everyone was busy telling their share of the story.

This irritation lingered within me as I kept thinking I forgot something but didn't know what or about what. My soul had stored lost memories that wanted to surface above the water and get back into my memory bank. The memories were flooding back, yet I couldn't catch them. A huge wave crashed onto our ship. I felt like there was something scratching my head, but I couldn't get a grip on it. I let the feeling wash away and focused on what was really in front of me, not what I assumed was in front of me.

A crew member was busy talking as he said, "The rumored queen of the island from whom the island found its name sucks people into her web. If someone gets into her castle even by mistake, they are never ever seen again. They vanish and don't exist anymore. I am telling you all, I will not enter that castle! I have a family waiting for me back home."

I heard his words but decided to stay quiet and not speak. Everyone has a voice and the freedom to be employed or quit and not be employed. Everyone in my company has free will and works by choice. I made a mental note and decided to get all new crew members on my next trip. I would need to make sure everyone knew and signed a waiver before coming aboard. My company would have to bear all the expenses for any crew members to return and for new crew members to come.

The rustling ocean waves moved like a graceful lady floating away. The waves became loud as they crashed against the huge ocean boulders. It was then I stood up as I heard and saw the water which then looked like a very elegant lady screaming in anger. She was screaming not because she was at fault, but why the boulder was in her way.

On the upper deck of the cruise ship, I stood mesmerized by the vast and rough ocean water, the ocean breeze, and the huge white goshawks which were all white with dark red eyes, yellow legs, and yellow feet flying in the sky above.

From the cruise ship, I saw a small human population on the rocky beach. I also saw whales and seals floating freely like they were in their own haven. Without any binoculars, I saw a pod of bottlenose dolphins jumping in and out of the water. An island that people said didn't exist was there in front of me, as if whispering in my ears she is very real. The mysterious island was watching me. Somehow, I also felt like from the beyond someone was observing me. I didn't know if I enjoyed the feeling, or I absolutely dreaded the horrific touch of eeriness.

We were still in the water and could see the island. I realized this part of the ocean belonged to the island. Abruptly, the ocean churned, and the water level rose like we were going into a tsunami. The trees that were visible on the island were all announcing there was a storm brewing in the water, the land, and the skies. A perfect sunny day for a few minutes disappeared as we all saw ourselves within a very paranormal storm. I tried to keep calm as I kept hearing, "You are back!"

The unnatural storm disappeared as abruptly as it had appeared. The very quiet, only talks or responds when directly questioned, captain of my ship sailed past the dolphins to stop at the triangle-shaped island. From far away, it looked like a vast amount of land with some hills was just floating in the middle of the ocean. I wondered if it was real or a mirage. After we docked at the island, I realized the island was real and the castle I saw from far away really sat there on top of a small hill. From close, the castle didn't seem that big or threatening as it did from far away. It too somehow spoke to me and told me all about her and her past, the past I chose to forget.

I reminded myself dreams are just another world, not my world nor my reality. I felt shivers run down my spine like I never did before. The trip, the island, and the castle felt weird and for the first time in my life, I hoped I wouldn't regret this purchase. It was like a fatal attraction against my own cold feelings. My dreams that flooded me every single night were all about her.

The same song she kept singing in my dreams, she was now singing for everyone to hear,

"It's only me and you.
It's only about us.
It's only our love story.
You chose to forget.

You drowned everything with yourself,
Although you promised
Never would you
Ever forget
As it's not just a love story.
It's our immortal love story."

Everyone heard the musical words being sung in the air. The rough winds joined her. My crew members were in shock as they heard her song and tried to hide within the ship's cabins. For some strange reason, my heart ached for her. I wanted to tell her not to cry because I had arrived. Many nights, I wished dawn would never come and the night would never end. With dawn, my dream would break, and like the mysterious island that disappears, my beloved dream wife would also disappear at dawn. Today, I hoped not to fear the feared one, but if possible, I wanted to ask her if it was she who visited me in my dreams and why.

I warned myself this purchase could have been a trap. It could have been a spider's web I was getting trapped in. Why was I attracted to a ghostly woman who called me in the middle of a dark ghostly night? Was this the same woman who visited me in my dreams? In my dreams, she called me her husband and said it had been too long. She said the separation had become deadly for her. I laughed as I woke up thinking isn't a ghost already dead? So, why was she afraid of death? Maybe there was some hope that she was alive and not dead. I tried to shake off all the feelings and would let my awakening state's judgment rule, not my dreams alone.

The island spoke to me as I heard the winds carry to my ears a woman's trembling voice, "Welcome home. For thousands of nights and a thousand years, I have been awaiting your arrival. For thousands of nights, I have tried to call upon you in your dreams. Please come closer so I can sense you, so I can smell you, so I can feel you, but I cannot see you unless you enter my home and touch me. Oh, my darling, you are finally home. Please remember the dreams and don't judge them without remembering me, and our immortal love story."

I ignored the words as after being in the water for days, even mermaids would seem real. This island was never touched by cyclones or tsunamis. There were a lot of small colorful cottages, modest shops, and a lot of boats floating as shopping markets. The marketplace had so many souvenirs for the tourists to find. A waterfront boat also worked like a floating school for the children of the island. I saw the schoolteacher, my childhood buddy whom I knew very well, wave at me. Everyone on the small island was happy to see my ship come to shore.

It was very clear they were all waiting for me. The students were dismissed from school, and all went walking home with their parents. The island was small enough for everyone to walk around yet there were tuk tuks and tractor-drawn wagons. It didn't look mysterious but like a small island full of life.

The schoolteacher wearing khaki pants and a khaki shirt walked toward my cruise ship which had docked with the help of a lot of islanders. I knew the weather was nice during the day yet cooled down significantly during the night, so I was well equipped with all my necessities. I kept a small cottage on the island for my private use, aside from the castle, as my buddy convinced me to do so. He had said this was the only place on Earth I would not be bothered by anyone and could concentrate on my upcoming books.

I intended to enjoy my quiet days in serenity and the cool nights watching the stars and dolphins. I was looking forward to a nice cool winter. It was June, the start of winter which would end in August. The summer months are from December to February.

Dr. Linus Didáskalos, my childhood friend who invited me to this island, walked toward me with a strange disbelieving smile on his face. I wondered if he was smiling or if he was upset or angry. My friend always made the same face whether upset or happy and never showed his feelings on his face. He was a renowned Doctor of Parapsychology, and his life's research was proving the existence of paranormal phenomena. He believed in the after-death communication, medium and ghostly apparitions, dream communication, mind over matter, and the other things general humans can't see.

He made it his life's goal to find out more about the paranormal world. He always believed there is more than one world where we live side by side, but we just don't have the ability to see one another. Maybe one day, some people might have this power, and his life goal was to find them. So, he traveled to this mysterious island trying to prove his point.

As one of the world's top renowned geniuses, aside from his own passion, Linus chose to devote some of his time teaching poor underprivileged children basic foundational education, including literacy and numeracy. He traveled to the children who couldn't afford any kind of education and guided them through the first steps of schooling. He moved to this island to sit in the open air and maybe if lucky do both, teach the children and learn more about the paranormal world.

Linus believed if knowledge and sources were limited to the children, then the teachers should travel to the children and give them the needed knowledge. Recently, he had gone missing. His ship disappeared and we had no contact with him for eight months. The search for his whereabouts stopped after six months of trying to find him. I hoped and prayed if we couldn't go to him, maybe through his paranormal research or belief, he could come to us.

It was only two months ago Linus contacted me, but he sounded so different. He informed me how he had tried to hide himself away from all the troubles of life and work on research quietly. His mother and I both knew about this and gave him all the needed space. Yet over the past month, he stopped calling me or his mother. It was as if he returned to the island and forgot he had a mother, an aunt, and a buddy back home on the mainland.

I found it strange that he didn't even ask about his mother, whom he never left alone and always made sure she was taken care of. A few months before he disappeared, he married the woman he met. Those of us on the mainland were all on the phone with him during the wedding ceremony. We all planned to celebrate when we came to the island. He got married on the island and soon after, he told everyone that he and his wife were expecting their first child. He was going to come to the mainland, but that was the last contact we had with him before he went missing. It had been months since I had seen Linus, so I wanted to inspect in person to see what was going on with my buddy.

As I watched Linus come near, he looked a little different. The aura around him was not warm but eerie. On the most recent phone call, he told me he had an accident and didn't want his family or friends to know about his accident or surgeries. Same face, same build, but I wondered why my best friend looked so different, like a different man. He was insistent I come to the island and said it was urgent.

Linus nodded his head up and down as he said, "Really? Lysandros Ealdwine, the famous author accepts my invitation and comes to the hidden Dead Queen's Island? Can I ask you though, why on Earth would you buy that haunted castle after I had personally forbidden you to buy it? That's the only place even the brave, friendly, and knowledgeable indigenous people dare not enter. For a thousand years, this castle has remained empty."

Linus was talking so differently from his regular self. I wondered what happened after his wedding that he had changed so much. Also, he looked healthy, but he had told me he was involved in a big accident after his wedding. Linus had dark frameless sunglasses on. They were so dark that I could not see his blue eyes. I tried to inspect him closely because he was walking differently. He was so smooth and elegant. I wondered where my very clumsy and accident-prone buddy was.

In a teasing voice unlike himself, he then said, “I know you’re a billionaire and can buy whatever you want. So, I say, buy castles, ships, islands, if you so choose. Simply please avoid that castle. It’s haunted and is cursed. Even though you bought it, you will stay in the cottage you also purchased solely for your personal use. I have arranged for you to be at both places. I won’t enter that castle unless you insist and invite me to do so, and as your best friend I would have to accept. I can’t let you go into that haunted castle all alone.”

I don’t know why I burst out laughing. I had heard the rumors of this castle being haunted. The real estate agent disclosed all the details and said he knew nothing about it as he never entered the castle. I had to buy it at my own risk with my sane mind and accept everything inside of the castle and on its grounds. The previous owners never set foot inside. Even the renovators refused to work there, giving the excuse that no one wanted to work on a remote island that appeared every thousand years.

The agent said a lot of investors were interested in coming to this magical island. No one wanted to enter the castle in fear they would encounter and upset the queen who had ruled this land. Through my research, I couldn't decide if people loved her or feared her. Everyone on this island still paid their gratitude and thanks to the Dead Queen who let all her subjects live here peacefully.

Somehow, the islanders were all provided for with fruits and vegetables no one planted or grew. The produce always came from the castle grounds and was left on everyone's porches. The most beloved and most feared queen still resided there even after her horrific death. No one entered the castle since the previous owner, King Villainous, passed away.

I watched my friend who was sweating like he was hiding something. No matter the season, Linus always looked like he had gotten a tan. As I observed up close, he looked fair, not his usual tan self. He looked like himself even after the surgeries but was missing his joyful personality.

I told Linus, "Yes, my dear friend, you are invited to enter my castle. Don't worry about any haunted castles as I don't believe in ghosts. Like us humans with a mission, the dead are entities that too have a mission. I don't fear the dead. I'm the one they should fear. Also, if anyone has been hiding in that castle for a thousand years, I would love to know how they lived for so long. Their longevity is a topic I would love to learn from. If they are dead, then it's good as I'm still alive. They should fear me, not the other way around."

A woman with long brown hair and fair complexion came from within the crowd and was listening in on our conversation. She kept pinching Linus as he either ignored her or didn't feel her pinches. She tried to check the castle from behind as she moved backward. She had a white bohemian dress on. The dress had a smocked bodice, long ruffled sleeves, and landed just beyond her knees. She had white sandals on and carried a shawl over her shoulders. She was ready for the cool night that would touch the island as soon as the sun set. She held a basket with freshly baked bread and churned butter. I could smell the bread and butter, and I realized how hungry I was. Linus stared at the bread and moved backward.

He kissed her head and smiled at her as he hugged her and said, "My beautiful wife, Alala, is the only reason I decided to settle down here rather than float around the globe like a lost soul. She is pregnant and still refuses to travel to have the baby. We'll probably go to Tasmania when she is ready though. That's where her parents are. Even they can't take Alala away from this island. The ghost of the castle couldn't get rid of her either. My wife at times accepts the bread sent from the haunted castle. Just like the Dead Queen sent when she was alive, she still sends bread and butter now."

Alala watched me as if she was trying to read my mind. She didn't speak for a while. We walked toward their beachfront cottage. It was a beautiful stone cottage with a fenced garden area where flowers bordered the property. A swing sat in the corner under a flowering bush. The cottage was big on the inside, and it was framed with a covered wraparound brick porch. The ocean breeze cooled the home. There was a huge double-sided wood-burning fireplace to warm the home during chilly nights. The fireplace was open to the porch and to the family room, which was strange. I wondered whether unwanted animals could enter the home if the door to the fireplace was ever left open.

I followed them into their parlor room which was small and functioned as a guest-receiving lounge. The room opened to a combined living and dining room. The cottage was very welcoming and set up as a family-friendly home, where one could walk in and help themselves to hot-cooked meals or maybe find a room to just take a nap as the bedrooms were all visible and open to a wraparound veranda.

A helper wearing an apron walked in with tea and biscuits. She set up everything on a butcher block dining table. I watched Alala give the helper the basket of freshly baked bread and butter. The helper saw the bread, bowed her head toward the castle, and remained quiet. It seemed all the cottages on the island somehow faced the castle. It mattered not where your home was, you would have a view of the castle as it sat on the highest point of the island. The helper glanced at Linus, and I saw a strange communication gap going on there.

The woman was making weird faces as she tried to inspect Linus. She kept touching her cross necklace she wore over her apron. I tried to read her mind, but I was worried why she was trying to read Linus's mind. Either the woman hated my friend, feared him, or they had a secret between themselves. I said nothing but with a PhD in psychology myself, I knew something was missing. I would pursue this at the right time.

Alala then with her Australian accent said to her helper, "Please set the table for three tonight. My husband's friend will be joining us. Also, take two loaves of bread and a jar of butter home with you for your family. My husband no longer eats bread or butter that comes from the castle like he used to. He has been acting strange ever since he came back. He didn't even bring his mother like he said he would, but he came back the same day saying he wanted to be with me."

The helper smiled, gave a very stern look at Linus again, and left the room. She was a happy-go-lucky woman who skipped out with the basket.

Then, she walked back into the room as she said, "My name is Ms. Baker. Are you the new owner of the haunted castle? If so, please take a jar of salt with you when you go there. Or maybe you can stay in the cottage next door and just avoid the castle. Anyone who enters that castle never comes out ever again. Also, I have sprinkled salt around your buddy and maybe you should too. I don't like him, and I'm scared for you. Why would you knowingly buy a haunted castle?"

Ms. Baker walked out with a frightened face. I wondered why as I never said anything about the castle or if I would move in or not. All the talk about the hauntings though attracted me toward the castle. Somehow, I was pulled even more toward it. It was as if I could hear a sweet voice singing from the castle that was so mesmerizing to me. I didn't want to waste any more time but just wanted to go there. A magnetic pull was calling me, and I had to struggle with all my might to stay steady on my feet.

Alala observed my face as she asked, "Why do you keep staring at that castle like you are being pulled toward it? Were you aware about the horror stories when you bought the castle? Even then, I hear you're rich so just keep it but don't go there. You will never get any help or gardeners or workers to work there for you. Listen to this sister's wise words and don't go there. It's haunted. Everyone loves to see it, talk about it, and even show it off to the island's visitors. Yet no one has set foot in it for a thousand years. The mystery is how it is still standing and who takes care of it. The owners before you never visited this castle. You would be the first one. We, the people of the island, take the gifts from the castle as a friendship offering, and that's it."

Alala walked in front of her husband as they wanted to get a closer look at the castle, but she almost tripped. Linus didn't move as if he too was mesmerized by the castle and just stared at it. I knew Alala might trip as the flooring in these older homes were not level. I ran and held Alala from the back to support her. She said nothing as to why her husband seemed so distanced. I wanted to say so much to my friend but stayed quiet for I never intended to get in between a married couple.

The weather was changing as the clear blue sky rumbled, the blue ocean churned, and suddenly without any sound or warning, lighting struck next to where Linus and I stood. No one screamed or was bothered by the strange phenomenon. I watched them and said nothing like all right if it's so normal for all of you, then it's normal for me too. I stood up and saw the castle was very visible from the whole island. Everyone could see the building, so maybe the ghosts of the castle could see everyone from their hidden gothic tower.

Ms. Baker came back and served freshly cooked red beans and rice, and baked fish with fried plantains. We started with avocado salad and freshly baked bread and butter. The meal was amazing. For dessert, we had cut fruits. The bread melted in my mouth and somehow, I remembered the taste. I knew I had it before.

Ms. Baker then said, "The bread and butter are her gifts. We all love it and have not died from it yet, so I'm saying it's safe to consume. She is still in that castle. At night, everyone hears her cries and screams. She has been haunting this castle for as long as I can remember. Don't go there. She has been waiting for someone and will only leave when she finds him. Please stay away from the haunted castle. Don't start a war you can't finish, please. And where did Mr. Linus go? He didn't touch his dinner."

I wondered why everyone was so scared of her castle. If the whole island was named after this same ghost, then why did she only haunt the castle, not the island? If she was so bad, then why was she still providing for everyone even after her death? I thought about how my captain and the crew members with the ship left to get supplies and things I needed from India. Because of the distance, the journey by water would take them a few weeks to return. My clothes were all drenched from sweat but I felt cold and would have loved a sweater.

I said out loud, "So, this island, the Dead Queen's Island is named after the same ghost of the castle. Then, why doesn't she haunt the island but only people who go to the castle? She had to enter the island to go to her castle when she was alive, so even in death she could come to the island if she so wishes. I wonder why. I will go to my house as now it's not the Dead Queen Maharani Aarna's castle but Lysandros Ealdwine's home."

I tried to see the castle through my dreams. I closed my eyes and thought of my dreams and my dream wife. Did my dream wife and this woman have anything in common?

The longing of the separated lovers splashed a very cold dose of icy feelings within my inner soul. Somehow, I wanted to rip apart all the missing storylines and get to the end of the story. As an author, I always write the ending first, but here in reality, I would need to walk through life to get to the end of this mystery.

The cold feeling of longing for someone I didn't know but so much wanted to be with gave me the shivers. How did I know the name of the Dead Queen? No one asked me as they all assumed I must have read all about the mysterious woman. So, that's how I knew her name was not Maharani but Aarna, which in Sanskrit means wild forest or the jungle woman, maybe because she was wild.

Or did she have all the answers to my questions as her name also means the answers? On the island, people knew her as Maharani, but in my knowledge that's a title which means the great queen. When she died, she was known as Maharani, and so, her house was known as the Dead Queen's Castle.

THE DEAD QUEEN'S CASTLE

The Dead Queen
Stands by the ocean.
Her lost love
Is lost within
The ocean
Of the lost,
As her longing,
Her yearning,
And her emotions
Tear and rip
The land,
The ocean,
And all
Around her.
She calls her beloved
Through sweet songs,
Through tears,
And through
Agonized cries.
For a thousand years,
She has been calling,
Never giving up,
Never going away,

Never letting go
Of her love story.
No one
Wants to listen.
No one
Wants to see.
No one
Wants to remember her,
Her love story,
Or her agony
Of separation
As all are
Terrorized,
Threatened,
And intimidated
By the ghostly
Apparition
In
THE DEAD QUEEN'S CASTLE.

Chapter One:

Welcome Home, My Beloved

"Attracted to
fear, I opened my
windows when fear
knocked, yet little
did I know,
you have been
waiting for only
me to say,
'welcome home
my beloved.'"

Sounds of the rough ocean waves entered my room through the open windows. Traveling in a ship around the globe, I learned sounds travel faster in the water than in the air. The sound of the waves always relaxes my inner soul. Scientifically, it is said these calming results are from the alpha wave activation in the human brain. So, these sounds are replicated and are used in meditation.

My troubled and unsettled mind, however, couldn't settle down. I kept surveying my new castle from the windows of a cottage set up as my temporary home until my castle was ready for me. Yet would my unsettled inner temple sustain and keep my emotions under control during the time I needed to wait?

A song or maybe some kind of a familiar musical tune entered my temporary home. The musical tune reminded me of pain, agony, and a tortured love story. Or were they sounds of cries and painful shrieks? I couldn't tell. The quiet peaceful night shattered through the air as now there was a voice that sounded like a woman. It sounded like she was calling someone.

The lantern placed over one thousand years ago was glowing and spreading its mystical amber glow all over the island from the castle. I hoped it was not a love spell being spread all over the island for I knew I was attracted to that woman and the haunted castle for some unknown reason. Maybe I was pulled to horror love stories or just sad, grief-stricken lovers. Or maybe my weird mind thought the ghost Dead Queen just might be the same woman who haunted my dreams.

The castle's lantern started to glow like the moon from above the sky upon the roof of the castle. Again, like a lot of nights, the moon was covered in the dark shadows of heavy clouds. The light started to circle and glow. As a traveler by ocean, I had to learn the distress signals. I saw there was a mayday signal coming from the castle. Mayday in French is *m'aider* which means help me. The mayday distress signal was created in the 1920s, so how did our thousand-year-old Dead Queen know it? Maybe because she was around for a thousand years and was picking up on modern technologies.

Children and adults were all gathering up in groups. Parents tried to hold on to the younger ones. The dark night lit up with lanterns in everyone's hands. Some had long walking canes, some had machetes, and others had axes in their hands. I wondered where all these people were going with their garden equipment.

A person in the crowd with a priest's clothes on and a huge cross in his hands, said to Linus with a quivering voice, "Dr. Didáskalos, are you awake? Please do something. She is out tonight but there is no full moon out tonight. She is singing again, and I worry if something goes wrong. We accepted the bread, fruits, and vegetables as peace offerings for a thousand years. Ever since you have come everything, has changed as if she has awakened. What have you done Dr. Didáskalos? Why does she seem furious?"

The man was elderly and had a priest cap. From the glowing lantern of the castle, I could see he was sweating even on a chilly night. He was shaking his hands up and down as he spoke. He looked like a very nervous man who was overfilled with anger. I was worried looking at him panic. What if he had a heart attack? He was obviously scared. He held on to another man's hand who I thought also was a priest but blind as he was walking with a cane and needed help to get around.

I walked outside in the courtyard as did Linus and his wife Alala. The moon was out but not visible as it was covered by the clouds. I loved walking under the moonless skies as a young lad. Somehow, I would imagine the moon got shy and hid herself as my beloved and I were out trying to make love. Yes, I did ask the moon how many love stories she had witnessed. She never answered as I assumed she gives all lovers privacy to write their love stories. I often told her, how much I adored her for keeping a full diary on so many love stories but keeping them hidden in her chest. If only I could have read my own love story sacredly stored in her chest. I appreciated the miraculous wonder of the amazing glowing moon of my God.

I jolted back to reality, however, seeing the glow from the lantern reflected in the ocean. Like a mirror, the ocean was glowing magically. The castle's reflection could be seen enchantingly in the ocean water. Even the high tides and the moonless darkness couldn't erase the image of the magical castle from beneath the waters. Like a magical mystery, even the ocean was testimony to all the love stories that were written within her reflection.

I asked myself if time could just freeze and we could all be with our beloveds for eternity. Yet I took a deep breath and realized all the love stories and all the lovers were divided by a single breath. The bridge of life and death stood in between twin souls. Maybe the bridge of division would evaporate and open up the invisible gate for all twin flames to unite one day.

There in the mirror of the ocean appeared a transcendent enchanted queen, wearing a black gown, with a crown that glowed like magic on her head. I couldn't see the entire crown, but there were sparkles on it. Maybe it had a special type of shining stones. The windy night's winds did not touch or blow her hair. The ocean water did not wet her clothes as she was only a reflection in the ocean water. Or maybe, she was an underwater queen who lived beneath the ocean and roamed above the water to scare everyone.

She sang now so clearly,

"Float within the petals of a lotus,
Oh, my beloved.
Rise from the ashes,
Like an ember,
Oh, my darling.
I know you will arrive.
Riding upon the promises of true love,
You will arrive.
You will carve a boat for me
Within your heart,
And I will be free
As you and I unite
Through the promises of eternal love.

One thousand years have passed
As I still wait for you to return.
Our love story will not be
Submerged under water,
As we will unite above
And beneath the Earth
With one another."

The woman started to cry and scream at the same time. Her agonizing pain of separation from her beloved brought tears to my eyes. I was shocked beyond my understanding why I was crying for a ghost queen, who was very openly terrorizing my island. Yes, I not only bought the castle, but not known to everyone, I also bought the island.

The skies were lighting up like there were fireworks. Birds were flying in a group trying to flee this horrific event. There was no rain or high wind in the air, yet things were moving from one place to another. The inhabitants of the island were all screaming in fear. People started to run in different directions, hurting each other, and falling on top of one another.

The island stores were usually open twenty-four hours because tourists arrive on boats at all times of the day or night. Every single shop sold big and small replicas of the haunted castle. They had posters and key chains of the ghostly castle. The businesses had taken advantage of the haunting stories and were profiting through the rumored stories. Tonight, even the small souvenir shop doors were all left ajar as their owners ran away in fear. I knew everyone would come back in the morning as this fear only ripped people apart at night. During the day, people would forget everything and go back to their ordinary life.

Women left their sandals and ran barefoot to run faster. Men discarded their hats and scarves so they could see where they were going. Even the children dropped their toys and books as everyone ran with their lives. I wondered if this was a regular event for everyone, as they seemed very efficient in how they ran to safety.

A young boy around seven years old pulled his mother by her hands. His small chubby hands were red from trying to save his mother. With all his might he kept pulling his mother's hands. I stood there and admired the love and bond of a son and his mother. I looked at the castle and wondered what kind of a queen are you that you have fun petrifying even children?

He looked at the ghostly apparition directly and with his childish voice said, "No, you bad woman! I am not scared! Get lost and don't hurt me or Mama. I will grow up fast! I will eat all my vegetables from now on and I will be stronger than you to make sure you never ever hurt my Mama. Go away and stop scaring us. I will buy a sword and make sure you are forever gone."

The child was wearing his Superman pajamas. He had on his head a hat with the castle's picture hand drawn. I saw him clearly as he had brown hair, brown eyes, and a milk mustache. In his hands, he had a cross necklace and a keychain with the castle on it. He lifted his cross and shoved it toward the woman. He kept his cross in his hands and raised it above his head. When he bumped into us, he touched Linus with his cross. I watched my buddy jolt and squirm his face like he was in pain. Then, he walked away from the crowd and gave the young boy an angry look. I wondered why he did that to a young child. Maybe he feared real-life horror movies. I knew he wasn't scared of horror movies. He had made it his business to go and watch every single horror movie released on the big screen.

As Linus tried to shove the boy away, I got in between and told him, "Linus, he is just a child. By God, what is wrong with you? The cross gives him protection from all evil. Why would you shove him away? Rather than embracing a child and his faith, you tried to knock out his blessed cross."

Linus shriveled his shoulders and just looked in a different direction. I guess everyone seemed extremely stressed over the Dead Queen's ghost. I didn't understand all the fear. I wondered how these people were strangers to the Dead Queen and her activities if she was famous for being the Dead Queen. I, however, kept my focus on Linus as I thought his eyes were bloody red and his face was burning red with anger.

I said nothing and eyed the castle I owned. The Dead Queen's very long and cold hands had different kinds of rings on her fingers. The jewelry covered fingers were drenched in blood. The dark red blood poured from her fingers, showering like pouring rain on top of all who were in her way. The blood poured on land and the stream of red blood ran into the ocean and made the ocean water blood red. The ocean then created huge waves and brought red blood water from the ocean onto the land.

She said, "Hold me, my beloved. Carry me within your arms and take me away to the unknown land where all will say true lovers have united. For you, I have placed a blindfold and kept my eyes closed. We promised to only open our eyes when we unite again. Yet why did you break your promise when I have kept mine? I will open and see you only when you enter our home and touch me. Until then,

I am like a blind bride who waits for her husband to arrive and give her sight. Please hurry! I'm scared. Help me as these villagers and some very powerful people from these crowds are hunting me down, like I am a scary ghost or something. Please help me from drowning in the thirsty unjust anger of blood."

The woman was standing on top of the water with a black blindfold over her eyes. It was all so strange as in front of my eyes, I witnessed a ghost floating on the ocean who said she was scared and letting the world know she was afraid of someone too. She was trying to shake something off her fingers and hands. She was trying to jump up and down as she cried and kept screaming.

She kept saying, "Get it off! Wash it off! Please help me!"

Strange thoughts came to my mind. We all saw she was drenched in blood. Blood was dropping from her bloody fingers. So, why was she then asking for help? What was happening? I needed to ask the Dead Queen when we could meet, and if the dead fear the living as the living fear the dead. Only she would know. Yet again I asked myself, why was I not scared of her? The whole village who took her help for bread and butter feared even her shadows.

We all then saw she was standing in the tower room of the castle. She was wiping her eyes as she placed her head back up. She tried to see from her blindfold something but then she walked back into the castle with grace and poise. We could all hear she was still crying and cursing at the same time. Her musical voice was mesmerizing like how some might say, sirens cast spells. This mystical queen I thought did not place any such magical spells at least on me. I believed in what I believed, and no one could change my mind as I walked with scientific proof and the guidance of my God.

Yet my belief that ghosts didn't exist in real life might just change after tonight. I kept asking myself why her terrifying magical actions didn't scare me even when I saw her clearly. If anything, I was even more determined to enter my home. It's like when my mother would say to me as a child, not to take the hot oven-baked cookies and wait for them to cool down. I would run for it, burning my mouth and lips, yet glowing with pride I had hot oven-baked cookies. It was worth the steal and burn. So, I assume meeting you, my Dead Queen, eye to eye would be worth it. You're like the hot oven-baked goodies I want to get to the bottom of in this story. You, my dear, had been brewing for years.

The Dead Queen started to sing again with a very sweet voice as if she was ready to place everyone to bed. Maybe it was a lullaby or a magical spell which she used to calm everyone down after she got everyone agitated. She started to sing very sweetly like she could not even remember a few minutes ago she was the crying hot tempered queen.

Maharani said, “Has it been one thousand or two thousand years, my beloved, that I have not seen you? If I were a bird, I would hide in your neighborhood trees. If I were a cloud upon the skies, I would float above you to prevent the scorching sun from burning you. Oh, my beloved, I would remain as your umbrella eternally. If I were a road, I would let you walk upon my chest and maybe calm my temper and worries away. Yet I am only a human with no heartbeat. You, my beloved, are a human with heartbeats. Yes sweetheart, we are separated by only one heartbeat. Oh, my beloved, my soul calls your soul. I know you will arrive riding upon the love boat of our memories, only to save me, as then our love story will triumph. So, I sing sweet promises from my soul to yours. The ocean waters can take them to you. Arrive soon for I have been waiting for thousands of nights. Please my beloved, remove the one obstacle we both have in common, as we are separated only by a heartbeat.”

I assumed she wanted her beloved, presuming it was me, to be with her on the bridge of death. I didn't mind if that meant my sweetheart and I would be together, but I didn't believe in taking my life or anyone's for that matter. So, my beloved would need to wait until my days on Earth are over. For my twin flame, I would wait until my time on Earth is over. That much I could promise.

The crowd got bigger as the moon started to play peek-a-boo from behind the clouds. The Dead Queen disappeared like fog. I wondered who was she? Why was she scaring the islanders away? I heard people were leaving the island for the same reason others were arriving by boat, to get at least one glimpse of the Dead Queen. She provided for them but also scared the people to the point that their souls were trying to leave their bodies. It's like the deadliest scariest stories that give people the shivers still attract people to them.

I saw people fainting all over like we were playing a game of who can fall first. The family members were all scattering around trying to take their fainted family members back to their cottages. It's strange how people think they can just walk into their homes and close the doors, as that will keep the troubles outside. All around the oceanside, fainted bodies were being spotted like seashells. It seemed like everyone just wanted to camp out by the ocean. I walked and saw there were only adults lying on the ground fainted.

The little children were sitting by their parents, grandparents, and older family members. They were laughing how the brave adults couldn't take the drama, but it didn't bother the children. I tried to wake up as many as I could. The children started to panic and were crying as they realized this was not a game and that their parents really had fainted.

They all screamed and were saying, "Game over! Let's go home!"

The children all were asking everyone for help. I ran toward as many as I could. Ms. Baker and Alala came and tried to help me. It was disheartening to see adults who could have helped just walk away with their youngsters, not giving any helping hand.

A little girl with huge dark brown eyes and black hair stood by me and said to me, "I am from India. We're vacationing on the island. Mama and Papa wanted to see the Dead Queen, but why did they faint? I'm not scared of her. She is so beautiful and has hair like me. Maybe she was an Indian princess like Papa calls me. Do you think she is a real Indian princess who came here and is stuck? You should find a horse and giddy up to her and help her. Maybe you're a prince or a king or can become a king. Oh well, then beware. There is always an evil character in each story hidden somewhere. I love it! I'll wait for Mama and Papa to wake up."

The little girl smiled and kept playing with the sand. She was busy searching for seashells. I wondered how children play even at these late hours. Alala came and helped her as she woke up her parents. Ms. Baker was busy trying to help as many as she could. She thought all troubles could be fixed with a hot bowl of soup and freshly baked bread. She was offering to everyone this meal which was going to be prepared at my cottage.

That's when I turned my attention to the anger-filled voices of people I had never met and had never known existed. All of them were shouting at the same time, complaining how they were all scared to bits, and it had to be my fault. They said I awakened her by purchasing her castle. They all unitedly placed the blame on my head.

A woman shouted in fear and was stomping her feet. She was shaking and looked like she was about to join the group of fainting people. I didn't know if she was pretending to be awake or pretending to be fainting, but she looked like she was pretending either way.

With unjust anger and excessive rage, she shouted, “My little ones don’t sleep. They don’t go to the bathroom without someone accompanying them. This isn’t the kind of life we asked for. We’re going to leave. We stayed for Dr. Linus Didáskalos and his family so we could change this island into a home for us who live here and welcome visitors. He had said his friend, a rich man, had bought this whole island so we don’t have to worry about paying rent. We just had to work for his family and run this island. Tourists were coming and we would all have a life in paradise. It seems like we will all end up in Heaven soon if we stay here.”

The woman shook her head and tried to lift her child up, but the child wanted to be free from being held. The little boy had a huge smile on his face like he just won a battle. As I winked at him, he winked back at me with a huge smile. The mother, however, missed everything.

She said again like a broken record, “It’s too much for my heart and my husband’s. Whoever bought that house has started all of this. I know you can’t be the billionaire who bought the island, but it’s rumored you bought that castle. Why? I only ask you the rich people, don’t you have castles and estate homes in your own towns? Why do you come here when you can go anywhere? We can’t afford to go anywhere but must leave because of the rich and famous people’s fun and games at any cost. Yes, we get a life of free rent and school and a lot of privileges, but we didn't ask for a ghost to be included in the package deal."

She had her anger matched by hitting the ground with her hand. She just fell to the ground and joined the group of fainted people. I knew she was pretending as she kept pulling on her children who wanted to be free from her.

Ms. Baker walked up to the fainted woman and pulled her by her hair, made her sit, and said, "I can't believe my ears. You're a lying culprit. You came to this island to escape a prison sentence. You are wanted for thieveries. How dare you blame it on one person! This has been happening for a thousand years. She comes and goes and every one of you know what you got yourselves into. Did you sign a deal which said there were to be no ghosts included in the deal? No, you did not. The vacationers came to see her, the ghost woman. The workers are all here because the island is rumored to be haunted. Because of her rumors, you all have a job. You just lied and you know what? You all might be fired and sent back to your homes by morning. If the owners of this island find out what you have said, you are for sure to be on your way home by morning. Now go on, sprout, go home, and get lost. Let us the islanders sleep."

I was happy no one linked me to the billionaire owner of the island. I like to be known as the man who sits and walks with all walks of people. I was glad they all thought I just bought the castle not the whole island. I couldn't blame Ms. Baker. If my mother ever found out about any of this, she would have these people removed even if I asked her not to do so. I would, however, try my best not to get anyone fired. I loved Ms. Baker. She was one tough woman. She wore her hand-embroidered white nightgown that made her look even more elegant. I was now forever an admirer of Ms. Baker. Somehow, I was able to wipe off everyone and all the conversations from my head.

As thoughts of the Dead Queen seeped back into my mind, I wondered did she then not sing every night? Did all of this start after I bought the castle? Or since the arrival of Linus? Very disappointing my dear ghost queen. Here little ghost queen, I wondered how you knew I was here, singing for only me and thinking of only me. How could I be so lucky that a beloved of mine from one thousand years ago would still sing and cry for only me? No, it's all just my mind, thinking about my dream wife.

Okay, the horror romance got horrific as she was still singing. Amazing voice, but who was she calling and why? I just needed to tell these people something to calm them all down before they all brought my family name down. Why were all of them giving me the look? I wondered if I too looked like a ghost. I certainly didn't carry a poster saying hey, I'm the owner of this island. If I could, believe in me, I would hide from my family fame and name.

Anyway, if they didn't know my identity, then why were they all upset at me? Who appointed me as bossman? Yes, I knew money appointed me as bossman. They knew I had enough money to buy a haunted castle, so I must be rich enough to just waste money on a house I might not be able to stay in. I hate you Mr. Money. Again, I hoped I didn't open the portal to misery. Or did Linus open this portal by inviting me or coming here himself? How was Linus involved in all these ghostly affairs? Thank God, he didn't tell anyone about my family and my link to the island.

The screams all around me became louder and I wondered who was louder, the frightened people or the ghost woman everyone called the Dead Queen. The nightly prowlers were coming out as I could hear wild animals join the musical nightly sound. I had never liked wild animals, so I hoped I didn't get to see one.

I told all the humans on the ground and on their feet, "I assume this wasn't the first musical concert she has held. If you're so scared, why do you all wait for her? Why have you all never entered the castle? Why is it no one enters the castle and investigates why she is even there? Is she really a ghost which I know she probably is, but this still needs to be investigated. I have called the new owners of this island and all of you will be given free rides back home. The owners will invite all new employees who are not afraid of ghosts. I also did check, and it seemed like you all had signed a waiver about the ghost rumors."

No one was paying attention. Fear is one such thing that it grips people and takes away the liberty to move or talk as we would like to.

Yet everyone at once started speaking, "We don't want to leave the island. We are not scared, and we didn't have any problem with the owners of the island. We just don't like you and how you bought the castle. You have opened the portal to the ghost woman."

I tried to be relaxed and not expose myself as the sole owner of the island. I knew how to escape getting angry and just walk away as my buddy had always done that for me. Where was Linus and why was he acting so strange?

I very calmly said, "Also, how, why, and when did she become a ghost? These hauntings will stop when we have the answers to these questions. Or if you all don't want to investigate, then just enjoy the music, and go to sleep. Let me sleep. I don't fear ghosts but only the reason she is a ghost. Are you all not in the land of the living and she is in the land of the dead? So, why fight with her? She is stuck there, and you all are free to go where you want to go. For the record, the owner of this island has appointed me to investigate the ghost queen."

Quietness took over. Everyone started to smile and just walked away. Some ran as they hid their fears, and some walked calmly, or pretended to be calm. Suddenly, everyone just wanted to go home. Ms. Baker was giving to all who wanted to eat, freshly baked bread and bean soup. She smiled and served like a champion. I winked at her, and she winked back at me. The moon was glowing and made everything bright and clear.

I thought I must be good at speaking as everyone listened to me and tried to run in all directions. My joy and happiness did not last long. Suddenly, we were all soaked with ice-cold water from nowhere. The water soaked those who were running and those who closed their eyes and just waited for it. The ice-cold water felt like frozen knives were piercing into the skin. Yet as an author of so many gothic novels, research taught me this was our minds playing games and would pass shortly. The hardest part was letting time pass as the pain felt very real.

Again, no one cared about what I had said but they all knew what was coming. I was the only one who didn't, so I didn't feel bad getting wet. They all knew and still couldn't avoid the outcome. I saw my friend was looking at the skies above us like somehow, he was in a daze. He kept blinking in the pattern of the ice falling. I stood in front of him with my back toward him. I didn't want him or anyone else to get hurt because of me. If it was really my purchase that started all of this, then I would end all of this, my own way, in my own time. Linus touched my back, and I jumped as the hair on my back went up and I felt a cold shiver.

He said, "Wow, you do fear ghosts. I assumed you're fearless. Found your weak point, to touch you from the back. Anyhow, don't worry about the ice water. At least it wasn't rotten eggs, tomatoes, or rodents this time. It's getting worse as fear is something no one wants to live within. Maybe read a horror book or see a horror movie but to live within a never-ending horror novel is not something everyone wants to do."

We walked back to my cottage. Linus was walking so strangely. It was just weird. He was inspecting everything in the room which he supposedly had arranged before my arrival. The cold wind blew into the room as he jumped backward. I wanted to ask him if he was feeling all right. But

I avoided saying anything as I wanted to hear what he had to say.

He then continued and said, "You must have a peaceful resort ambiance because you bought this island to have peace and give peace to all your visitors. I assume you must be the billionaire who bought the island. This private island is completely yours. All the cottages are yours and all the rent payments will automatically go to you. So, my advice is you need fearless people to run the island. Try to get rid of the Dead Queen instead of investigating her. Just ask her to leave eternally."

I wondered what was wrong with my friend. I didn't buy the island on my own as it was his advice for which I purchased this island. What rent payments? Yes, I own it as the only child whom my mother gave all her family fortune over to. But I didn't want anything, and Linus knew this. I heard his words, but I felt uncomfortable especially regarding his advice that I should ask the Dead Queen to leave.

I also didn't enjoy how he was letting everyone know I was the billionaire who bought the island. I thought he had kept that part a secret. Yet it was strange as if he too was asking if I really owned it or not. Linus had personally arranged all the paperwork, and I signed everything in front of him. The islanders knew I own the castle and some businesses, but not the whole island.

I touched my friend's shoulder and told him, "I would very much appreciate if you could keep my name as the man who owns this whole island private. I only bought it so all these people could work and live here peacefully and for free. Their work would pay for their free living. I didn't do this so they would admire me. They all know about the castle but not how I am also the same businessman. I don't want any kind of fame or name, just peace."

I wondered why when someone spoke ill of the ghost woman, it hurt me so bad. Why did those words feel horrifying as if they were ripping me apart? All the ice-cold knives shooting from nowhere stopped. The night was still young as I kept watching the castle and knew I had to move in and end whatever was hidden within its walls. I planned to release the truth and walk into the history through the castle to stop all of this from happening in the present. Let the past be left in the past. Let the present be a surprise filled with gifts, and the future a blessing to all who end up there through the wagon of time.

The only way the horror could end was if I opened the doors and the windows of the past and welcomed everything bad or good through the windows of my memories tied to the castle, to the world. With fear or without fear, I knew I must do this. For this nightmare to end, I knew I must begin it again. So, I decided I would walk into the castle, open the doors and windows, and with that, I would open the doors and windows of my memories.

I called my business manager and waited for a while for him to answer the phone. He answered and in a very sleepy tone said, "Hmm, who calls this late? Is this a proper time to call? Do you know who you have reached? This is the company manager of the Ealdwine Family and Group."

On the side, I could hear his wife screaming and asking him to hang up the phone. She was upset at her husband as she said to him, "We don't need to have kids if you keep answering your phone in between. That's it! I can't do it anymore! Maybe divorce isn't a bad option. At least I can have a husband who wants to be with me, not look toward the phone to get away from me."

Okay the night was getting weirder. I interrupted a couple from having sex. I felt awful for his wife. Then, I wondered why they were forcing to have sex and didn't enjoy making love. In my heart, the first step in a relationship should be heart-to-heart connection. Then, everything else falls in place. Children or no children, twin flames should always be united through mind, body, and soul. I repeated to myself that it's none of my business. Not my love story, not my book, not my life.

I told my business manager, "This is Lysandros Ealdwine. As I recall, you are employed twenty-four seven with only paid vacation time. This is not your paid vacation period. You are still clocked on my time. I want you to get a team ready for me. I need security personnel, a team of twelve armed guards. Get a team of cooks, gardeners, house remodelers. You and your group need to be on the ship by tomorrow morning. If anyone can't be on the ship when my ship reaches land to pick you all up, consider yourselves fired. Also, get a team of new residents for the island who will sign all the necessary papers and who will be fully aware this island is haunted by the Dead Queen of the castle, for which the island is still known as the Dead Queen's Island. Anyone who disagrees here will accompany you on the ship going back."

I hung up and wondered if Ashok Mitra, my business manager, would come or not. I knew he and his wife were having troubles. He had mentioned he was blackmailed into a forced marriage he never had a choice in. I avoided personal matters and just let these things go out of my system. Things I couldn't do anything about, I breathed out and let them go as time would heal those problems. I've always liked to put all my effort into things I knew I could change if I tried. If I could financially or physically, I would help all who ask me for help. Yet I'm not a marriage counselor, so that's something I would avoid.

Alala hugged me and as she gave me a cup of lemon ginger tea, she said, "Maybe you were my brother in another life. In this life, I would like to be your sister, not just your friend's wife. Please stay safe. For whatever reason, I feel like you are pulled toward the castle. Just walk with your eyes open. It's your home, not hers. So, she can't be there, ghost or human. The castle was bought by you, so you are the owner. Remember, you are still alive and whoever she is or was, she is now dead. So, don't fear her. Let her fear you."

Alala was pregnant and somehow, I felt like she was sad. Maybe it's her pregnancy hormones or all the horrific events going on around us. I kissed my new sister's head, and I winked at my friend and signaled them both to go and rest for the rest of the night. I hope he saw my signal, but somehow, he was absent as if here but again not.

I wanted to ask him what was going on, but later when I had him alone for a while. A cold feeling stabbed inside of my soul as if I was missing something. Linus's hair looked different. It seemed grayer than when I saw him last. He placed his hands backward and waved at me. The feeling bothered me so much. I didn't know why my best friend seemed different.

The castle lantern in the lighthouse was glowing again. I tried to see it from my cottage. Alala walked into her home with her husband. Their cottage was a few houses down from mine, on the opposite side. I could see it clearly from my window. These cottages combined would still not make my mother's mansion.

I felt alone for the first time in my life. Strange, I had wanted to be alone and write my novel, yet the loneliness that I cherished before I dreaded now. My racing heart wanted so many answers to all my questions. I opened the windows and tried to sleep on the rattan lounge chair in the living room rather than on my huge bed covered by a mosquito tent. Mosquito nets draped the bed in a very exotic way. There was a small bamboo desk, and white linen drapes framed the small cottage. Amazing blue, green, and white color palettes and bare whitewashed wood floors made this an escape to paradise. This was a paradise where vacation cottages and even a ghostly castle all fit into one escape package which seemed really perturbing.

I tried to ignore the hair-raising feeling on my back, yet my neck felt something and reminded me not everything was as it seemed. Was I to be scared of what was in front of me, what was not in front of me, or was the mystery wagon waiting for me to unlock it? Light was swirling in a circle. Vibrations triggered my ear drums to react. Everything somehow was linked to this circular object that appeared from nowhere.

It's then, the sound waves traveled within my cottage as I heard another song,

"Tonight, my beloved,
I wait for my groom.
Tonight, I stay awake and have daydreams.
I don't let the nightmares open my eyes
As open or closed, I see nothing.
I just know you have finally come.
Tonight, I create my own fate
As I wish upon a star,
Shining on top of the ocean blue.
Tonight, I welcome my groom.
Tonight, I sing to him.
Oh, my beloved,
Oh, my love,
After thousands of nights,
Tonight, I open my heart's inner window.
Dear beloved, even without my sight,

I see you through the sight of my soul.
I pray to my Lord,
Please let my love story not end.
Let us not be separated by a heartbeat.
Let this breathless body
Have sweet dreams of only you.
Oh, my beloved,
This cold, lifeless, Dead Queen sings
To your living and thriving
Mind, body, and soul as I say,
Oh, my darling,
I love you,
And say to you,
I've been waiting a thousand years.
Welcome home, my beloved."

WELCOME HOME, MY BELOVED

My heart keeps
Drumming
As my soul keeps
Singing
For her
Whom everyone fears.
My soul
Asks me
To find her.
I have been thirsty
For a thousand years,
Thousands of nights,
And thousands of days.
I have waited
For my beloved
To give me
The immortal
Drink of love.
I have opened
My chest
And have told her,
You my dear
Belong only

Within the temple
Of my love
As my heart seeks,
Asks,
And knocks
Every house
To find you.
Yet I know,
You are,
You were,
And shall always be
Safely kept
In my soul,
As my soul is
Your permanent home.
So,
I say,
WELCOME HOME, MY BELOVED.

Chapter Two:

Open Invitation

"Knock,
knock,
open please.
Without thinking,
I say, come in.
Then, I ponder,
without thinking,
did I just invite
the devil with an
open invitation?"

Time washes away all the pain and memories like the waves of the ocean wash away the sand and all the sandcastles built on the beach by visitors. How and why does time fly away? I wondered if anyone ever could or would stop time from rushing away. I always thought through memories, we could frame time to be immortal. Yet memories remain intact within the minds of those who hold them hidden and within the vessels of sacred hearts. I kept asking myself how could one fight with memories that have been lost through the tunnel of life? If only time was immortal like love.

Maybe one day, it will be possible to stop time and freeze it during the first wedding kiss as the priest says, "You may now kiss the bride."

How do you tell apart memories that are the complete truth and memories that are jumbled up wishful or fearful thoughts? All my life, I have seen prophetic dreams, yet the dreams always came to me through a tunnel or so I thought. The tunnel looked like a crown and all the nine stones on the crown glowed and pulled me into the tunnel.

I woke up again after dreaming about a woman who was drowning. I was trying to save the woman from the cold, freezing, dreadful, and deep ocean water. The currents were against us as we tried to hold on to one another. When I finally reached her, I saw something was shining and circling in the water, but I was hit from the back, and everything became dark. I felt the cold hands of death touch me. I wanted the hands of death to let go of me and let me be with my beloved. I only wished to save my beloved first. Then, I would gladly give my hands to the unjust hands of death.

I told the unjust hands of death, "I accept everything, and I ask you for forgiveness for anything I might have done wrong. I forgive the person who struck me from the back but please let me save my beloved."

The memories felt like they were from yesterday when I saved her from the rough and cold water. Something was rubbing against my neck as I felt I was being strangled. Two hands held on to my neck as I could feel I was drowning and traveling to the bottom of the ocean. When a person drowns, the body floats and doesn't go deeper under the ocean. However, I was going deeper and deeper toward the ocean floor. I realized I didn't die from just drowning, but was strangled to death by my murderer, who too would have had to die to make sure I didn't float back. Why hate someone so much that you would wait for him to die and in the meantime, kill yourself too?

My nightmare broke. I was still frozen from the cold ocean water. My bed was drenched, maybe from my stress-induced sweat. With a lot of self-control and willpower, I opened my eyes and saw I was on the Dead Queen's Island, very much alive and breathing, not dead and breathless under the ocean. I could still smell the ocean water. My body felt tingly, itchy, and was burning from the salt water.

The name of the island bothered me a lot. Why would people call an amazing, beautiful, and peaceful island, the Dead Queen's Island? How could the Dead Queen have a peaceful island, after I assume a horrific death? Death, whatever way it may have been, was not peaceful if she was still haunting. It's my island now, so maybe we could have a name change.

I assumed the name attracted the tourists whom the remote island so much needed. The Dead Queen was like honey for the bees. It was a fantastic way to acquire all the horror-seeking vacationers. The islanders all sold items related to the castle and the Dead Queen. It seemed unfair they were profiting from her unhappy life story, yet they all feared her like she was a venomous ghost. I wondered if they were all trying to tease the queen so she would in return be angry and get them more customers. Or maybe the woman who was dead for a thousand years, was also playing games with them and refused to leave.

A vivid dream I had so many times from childhood was of a woman calling me. She had long black hair and kohl-lined eyes. On her head, she wore a circular shaped object with different colored stones. The stones were like torches that had forced me to close my eyes as even in my dream, I felt they would blind me. But again, I was never frightened of her.

I always saw myself drowning in the ocean, struggling to breathe. I wondered who the woman was and why I was in the ocean. From these snippets, I couldn't put the picture together. A sudden throbbing sound pierced my ears. I jumped up and saw Linus was calling me from outside of my door. I heard his voice which faded away as I fought to get up.

My mother had told me these dreams were from my imagination. I had always told her I would marry my twin flame after I find her from under the ocean. A young man's dream never did come true. All my life, I had repeated she lived under the ocean and that's where I would find her. I wondered why I was so pulled to the ghost woman who called for someone from above the ocean. I shrugged and reminded myself she was nothing but a pull toward the unknown mysteries I must stay away from. I must remember she was nothing but a figment of one's imagination.

A cold freezing hand touched my shoulder from the back. I absolutely hated that somebody touched me from the back as the memory of someone killing me from the back continued to haunt me. I jumped forward and banged my head on the window frame. Luckily, the windows were open, and I banged on the wood frame, not the thick heavy glass. Otherwise, there could have been some serious damage.

Linus was standing right behind me. He vaulted backward as he placed his hands above his head and said, "Okay, calm down. Maybe you should stop watching that castle and that ghost woman. Stop thinking about her. Stop looking for her. Stop calling her out. Ghosts can hear and might just pop in here. She hadn't come out of the castle grounds for a thousand years. Yet she was calling you. I banged on your door and your windows because you were screaming. Then, I just walked in."

Why would she be calling me? I must ask him. I rubbed my head and knew it wasn't bad he was there, but I wondered how I never heard him come in as if he too was a ghost. My childhood friend, I knew everything about him. He was a noisy boy and a very noisy and busy man. What was he doing here so late? I came back to reality and knew he was in my cottage. I was not in his home.

I looked at him directly and said, "How did you get into my home? I know I locked the doors and turned on the porch lights with security cameras. I heard no sounds, and the security alarms did not go off, so how are you in here? How do you say with so much confidence that the ghost woman is calling me? Did she tell you or were you with her in the past? She couldn't have told you tonight because she is in the land of the dead, and I know you are in the land of the living. Linus, just stop acting weird, okay? Shake yourself back to being normal. I miss my buddy."

Linus laughed and the whole house awakened with the sound of his laughter. It seemed like a horrific laughter, not my buddy's laugh. He was having a hard time controlling himself or was trying to avoid the talk. This was so not like Linus the man I knew. My friend had a hard time laughing in general. He was single and never dated anyone. He had said he would remain single until he madly fell in love and would invite the whole world at my expense.

He wrote to me about Alala and how she was his twin flame and would be with her in life and in death. His mother had not heard from him for a long time because he travels around the world and comes back when he wants to. His elderly mother was the one who reached out to me and insisted I should travel and find out what was going on and why he had gone missing. When we asked Alala, she sent a letter saying he was with her. He ended up not going anywhere because he was worried about her. Something just wasn't adding up.

I was confused how he ended up on a secluded island which he forced me to buy, then he either went missing or started to avoid me. I understand being a married man, he needed privacy. I loved his wife who was like my sister from another life. Yet who was this man standing in front of me? He was so different from my childhood friend. Again, I had a cold feeling. I wondered if I was still under water, and all this was a dream while I was drowning. My Linus was standing in front of me so everything would be all right. I just needed to shake away the unpleasant feelings.

I asked him again, "How did you get in here without the alarm going off, and so quietly? I'm here because your mother insisted you call her and at least let her know you're alive and haven't forgotten her. You're a married man, and you're having a child, so things are a little complicated. Why wouldn't you share this with her? Linus, shake yourself and just act normal. You're scaring me, Aunt Grace, and Mum!"

Linus stared at me for a while. I felt a cold chill in the air as if Linus had a cold aura around him. He stared at me as if he was inspecting my face. He laughed but said nothing. I shrugged the feeling off. I walked away to turn on the lights. I opened the French doors to the porch off my bedroom and let the moonlight pour in. The moon's glow made me feel like I had a friend watching over me. When the moonlight fell on Linus, he jumped backward. I almost laughed as I thought was he now a vampire? Maybe he married a vampire, and he too converted into one. That must be why he hated the moon's glow. I saw how he avoided the sunlight with his huge sunglasses during the day, but he still had them on at night. I wanted to pull off the glasses, but I said nothing.

I sat on the lounge chair on the wraparound porch which went from my bedroom to the living room and to the kitchen behind the house. The three-bedroom cottage was lovely with a study as a bonus room. It also had a basement that could be renovated if anyone needed more space. I loved how it was on the beach and was constructed to survive all storms. There were even flood walls.

Real estate development was my family's bread and butter. We had invested in islands and properties all over the world. We like buying small islands, making them self-sufficient, and converting them into resorts. I bought this private island. As part of the deal, I acquired all the vacation cottages, the shops, and the whole marketplace. This was a huge investment on my part, but a big help to this island community which was going bankrupt.

My whole team knew my name should never be known in public as the owner of the island. People should only know I bought the castle. I didn't have plans to change the island but keep the original buildings and character. Everything was modeled after a sandcastle and sand village I had built as I child. The island I had known from my inner soul. I didn't have to do much as everything was only façade renovations. I planned to keep the castle in its original form with minor renovations as no one wanted to go and work in that haunted castle.

Linus was watching me like he had not seen me in years, so I shrugged as he finally said, "I did not break into your home. Alala was worried because your windows are open and there is a storm coming. I have extra keys and an alarm code. I thought you wouldn't mind if I quietly walked in, closed the windows, and quietly left. Remember, you had invited me to enter and go as I wish into your cottages and castle. I only enter if invited. I can't go to places where I am not invited to enter."

What was he saying? He never needed an invitation to any of my places as we lived in the same house. We shared numerous family vacations together. I heard him talk, but then knew he was lying as there was no storm coming. I had just spoken to my ship's captain, our buddy, who was to dock in about two hours. He told me we didn't have any storms coming for a few weeks, so everyone on the renovation crew was on board with him. I kept the details to myself and said nothing to Linus.

I did, however, invite both Linus and Alala into my cottage. They were the ones who chose this cottage out of all the cottages for me. It was obvious none of them got rented quite often as the island was hidden and not known to many. I would have my crew advertise and change that situation. There was so much to do. I decided to stop thinking too much about why Linus was acting strange. He was my best friend, more like my brother. Maybe marriage changed him. If marriage could change a person this much that he forgot his best buddy, then I shouldn't marry.

Linus then said, "I would appreciate if you don't get in touch with my mother. We had a falling out about my wedding to Alala. Mummy didn't accept her and wanted me to give her some time. She had promised a maiden's hand in marriage to me when I returned. Everything was preplanned. So just don't worry about it. I will take my wife back home to Mummy after the childbirth."

His mother didn't accept Alala? What was he saying? I was there throughout everything Linus. His mother was excited and over the moon about Alala. She wanted me to take Alala and Linus back home so the baby and mother would be safe. I wondered if he was sleep talking and I shouldn't wake him up. I heard it was dangerous to wake up sleepwalkers. So, I stayed quiet. From childhood, however, Linus never sleepwalked. Why would he sleepwalk now? He never even needed any sleep. He would stay awake to do his homework and mine too.

Linus was in his own world as he said, "Now I'll go back home to my wife and tell her everything is all right. When you do go to the castle, please let me know. I would like to accompany you to the castle. We don't want the dead woman to get to you first, so I will be there by your side. When she sees you for the first time, I want to see her reaction. That's what friends are for. Also, who is Aunt Grace? Why would I want to upset anyone else?"

A cold freezing feeling seeped into my heart. I froze in spot and didn't even want to think about all the horrid thoughts that flew into my head. I froze in fear as to why did he ask, "Who is Aunt Grace?"

I watched Linus walk away from my cottage. As he walked from the porch toward his own house, he never looked back, nor did he make any sound as he walked. My buddy Linus couldn't walk without making a sound. We had fought many times about how his walks gave us away on the nights we tried to get out of the house quietly. I wondered when my childhood friend became so strange that it felt like I didn't even know him. Yet I still wanted my buddy to live and always in my lifetime to be alive and breathing. So, I tried to calm myself down.

His mother did know about Alala as she blessed them to be married quickly. We planned to do the reception on the island after he settled in. She was on the phone during the whole wedding ceremony. What was he talking about? The only reason she didn't attend was because she had a leg injury, which was what I was attending to and the same reason I also couldn't come. His mother didn't care about class or differences if he loved her. Why was he acting like he just jumped out of centuries ago? Maybe he had island fever and lost his memory. I should shake him up and just get him out of this sleepwalk stage.

I called him from the back and said, "Hey Linus, I don't mind you coming into my house even at the middle of the night. However, I do wonder when I'm married if my wife would complain. I wouldn't enter a married couple's bedroom or house in the middle of the night. So, I uninvite you from ever coming to my bedroom when my wife is here. Also, if you are asleep, then wake up. If you are dead, then get lost. If you are my Linus, again I repeat only if you are my Linus, then you are always welcome, dead or alive."

Linus stopped in his track and said without turning, "You can't uninvite once you already invite. Maybe then, you should avoid getting married. I'll come to your home anytime, anywhere, as you said, you don't mind. Thanks for the free invitation I was so waiting for. Also, who do I look like Lysandros? Look in the mirror and give me the answer. Let's hope your wife too invites me in. She too will see my reflection and yours in the mirror if you ever do get married. Maybe I will wait for your wife eagerly to finally come into the storyline because she will see my face as she will see yours too. I am waiting just for her."

The sun came up too soon. I tried to get some shut-eye, but could not. The lies of Linus bothered me a lot and I wanted to ask him so many questions. He couldn't remember his own mother's name. I couldn't tell Aunt Grace or my mother about this, because otherwise, they would send medical assistance over here immediately. Whatever was happening, I prayed it wasn't medical but maybe related to stress. Somehow, I thought it was better to give things their own time to dissolve. Yet I argued with myself against it, as maybe there was something going on I had no clue about. I decided to hold on to my thoughts until I had more reasons to investigate. I also wanted to wait until a doctor arrived.

My best friend Linus was raised in Tasmania, Australia as was his wife, Alala. I was also raised in Tasmania myself. So, his wife was not a woman from the mysterious island. He had wanted to marry her ever since his eyes met hers. My mother came from Greece, and my father came from the Netherlands. They decided to settle in Tasmania. I was born into money from my mother's side as the sole heir to her family fortune. My father gladly gave up all his fortunes and business matters to be with my mother. It was an eternal love story that ended too soon.

My father's death was unbearable, as my mother had gone into shock losing him right after my birth. She loved him and to this day, she says he is with her, and she feels him every second of her living life. Through memories, she kept him alive and for the memories, she still breathes. She learned to live life on her own, but for him, she never remarried.

My mother said I was born on a ship in this same water. My parents and Linus's parents were coming to buy this island. Both our fathers passed away in a tragic accident in the same ocean.

Linus's mother, a single widow, was my godmother. She raised me more than my mother who remained busy with her family business that gave us a roof over our heads. My mother's mourning time was lessened as Linus and I were born at the same spot our fathers had passed away. Our mothers had come to spread their husbands' ashes right after their deaths. Linus and I were both told we both must have died in the water in a past life as we were both born there. My twin friend hardly remembered anything. I wondered if the ocean was cursed, and if we should have avoided it.

Long before I bought the island, Linus had come home after a long vacation and insisted as he said, "We should buy that island. Our fathers passed away on their way to the island. We shouldn't be scared but celebrate their memories by buying the island. If you do invest Lysandros, I promise to help run the island for you my whole life and even after death. For some reason, I feel like I'm being pulled to the island."

Our mothers were against it but never had said no to us as they both knew we only wanted the family business to flourish. In my household, life and death are not to be feared as both our mothers taught us to accept the birth and death of a life as the will of God. You shouldn't challenge but celebrate God's will. A mystery that life accepts without ever challenging is the secret of life and death.

Never in my life did I hear Linus call his mother, "Mummy." He always called her, "Ma." Ever since I could talk, I called her Aunt Grace. My mother loved Linus's mother like a sister. They were together from before our birth and even promised to be sisters if God wills in their next birth. This conversation with Linus was freaking me out. I was going to call our company's doctor to the island as soon as possible. She would be able to take care of Alala and the baby too.

I knew Mum and Aunt Grace were still traveling for business, finding other small and remote islands to convert as self-sufficient resort islands. They had both decided against remarrying as they believed in twin flames and hoped they would both reincarnate only to be with their own husbands when it was time. I made up my mind that I wouldn't call his mother, but I would call my mother. If Aunt Grace picked up the phone, so be it.

My whole body was shaking in fear. I could barely feel my fingers when I gripped the phone tightly and I rang my mother. A soft and very shaky voice answered as I heard Aunt Grace's voice.

She was crying as she said, "Hello, hello, Lysandros. Oh my God, is this Lysandros? Where are you? Haven't you heard the news yet? Your mother Valery and I have sent you messages through Captain Anthony and your buddy Captain Dirk and Dr. Geeta who will be there soon. Everything is finished! I am devastated! We tried to call you, but the automated message kept saying you're in an area with no coverage. My Linus was murdered on his last trip! His body was found four weeks ago. I just received the dead body. According to the coroner, he has been dead for months, but his body was miraculously preserved by the ocean. Your twin buddy is no more. I promised I wouldn't cry, but it hurts so much. What do I do? I just need to hold you and feel you once my child."

I felt dizzy as if the Earth beneath my feet was lost. How could I go on without you Linus? We were born together, and you promised we would die together. It's not fair you beat me to this. I was born a few minutes before you. I spent my whole childhood and adult life with you. What happened? You fell in love and married overnight as we all celebrated over the phone. Then, you went to investigate and work in the newly purchased island. After that, you went missing, came back, and then you were murdered?

What happened? Oh my God, Alala! Who is she with then? Why and how did all of this happen? I realized my fingers were white and blue from holding my phone so tightly. I drifted off to an unknown world where I wanted to wipe off this truth and pretend this was all a nightmare.

Aunt Grace was still talking as she said, "I am lost with words but want to keep his last wishes alive. I want to come to the island with your mother and release his ashes in the water over there. He would then join his father and your father and be with them. I would feel better knowing father and son are together now. His father could not see him while he was alive, but in death, they can be together. Linus was so over the world with that schoolteacher's job that he never wanted to leave the island. He had told me that he wanted his wife to live with me because she so wanted to be with us."

Aunt Grace was crying, and I heard my mother try to calm her down. My mother was much more emotional over this as she had said so many times, Linus was really her son. She had told us over and over how she had nursed both of us. Aunt Grace couldn't nurse him because she got sick after her husband's death. My mother was strong and carried Linus and me. She also took care of Aunt Grace and the family business for so many years.

Aunt Grace was talking and broke my frozen state as she said, “Oh my God, what do I tell Alala? He said she is his twin flame, and he never wanted to part with her, his love, his life, his beloved wife, Alala. They married in a rush but wanted to celebrate the wedding after the child’s birth because she is pregnant. Lysandros, please don’t tell her anything yet. I would have never wished another woman on Earth to go through what your mother and I went through.”

Aunt Grace dropped the phone as I heard a helper try to console her. She was saying something I couldn’t hear, but I knew everyone in the household would be broken up into pieces over this intolerable incident. I needed to find out what happened.

Aunt Grace was trembling, and I could sense it in her quivering voice as she said, “We should be there in two days. Your mother is having a hard time dealing with this news, but I will survive. I will heal your mother back onto her feet. I believe God would not give me more than I can handle. So, I will not cry. Pray for your friend and please give me his wife and child so I can go on living through this unjust life after bidding farewell to so many of my beloveds. I worry as your mother and I are old. How long will we be able to take care of Alala and the child? Your buddy Dirk is going to be there to help with all of this. He too is broken up but said he will be strong for Linus. You stay safe Lysandros and maybe you can come back home with Alala and the child. Dirk said he will to his last breath take care of Linus's child. I know you will too for as long as you live."

The sorrowful hands of death were very strong around me. I needed to be strong for Alala. After I hung up the phone, it felt like the world was spinning around me. I forgot that I just lost my best friend. My twin brother from a different mother and father. My feet felt numb, and my head felt dizzy. All I could think was then who was the man disguised as Linus? How could he look identical? How was all this even possible? Was he an illusion the castle created to fool us? Who was he, and why was he staying in the house with my Linus's wife? I closed my eyes and placed my hands on my mouth as I rushed to the bathroom floor and cried my lungs out.

I told Linus in my mind, "How do I go on without you? We don't have a normal relationship. We were brothers from birth. You are the shoulder I leaned on. My shoulder was the wall you leaned on. Please tell me how I should go on living if you are not. You promised Linus, we would breathe together, and our last breath would be taken together. Come back to me and answer my question. I will rip apart the door of life and death and get you back or go to where you are."

I pulled my hair and tried to calm myself as I walked out of the bathroom. Yet I felt like vomiting as I ran to the bathroom again and splashed cold water on my face and my hair. I saw my face in the mirror as I remembered my buddy's face. I asked myself what the link was between us. This face of mine seemed so unfamiliar. How could I see my face and not yours? You always said you were handsome, and I was the weird one.

Without Linus by my side, I would feel lonely and weird. Without him, I would be incomplete. I wondered if I was the reason Linus was murdered. How did the maniac do it? I knew it from the first moment. How could my twin buddy not hug me or tease me or fight with me, like we always had. We would be pulling each other's hair, never giving up until our mothers intervened. Please Linus, hear me and come back. At least, tell me what to do.

When I saw the fake Linus for the first time, it was as if the universe had told me he was not Linus. For some reason, he didn't sound or feel like Linus. He seemed like a person who walked in from a thousand years ago. Oh my God, how would I tell or protect the very pregnant Alala, my

Linus's wife, and child, from this person trying to disguise himself as Linus?

I kneeled and said a prayer for my best friend out loud, "Oh my God, my Creator, I ask you to guide me through this storm of my life, not to save myself but the honor of my friend's wife and their unborn child. Please help me help her, and their child. Please help Linus and if it is even possible, guide him to me, so he can help me help his wife and unborn child. Please let the child be born safely. I ask You to either bring Linus to me or take me to him through the miracle of this prayer. You had created us together, sent us together, yet why have You taken him before me? My God, please help me get through this. I feel like I too have died and only my physical body remains. Please answer my prayers."

I walked out as I saw Ms. Baker walk toward my house. I made sure she didn't see any of my tears or hear my cracked voice. I wore dark sunglasses to cover my eyes. For some reason, I knew I had to be extra secretive.

Ms. Baker said, "You look weird. What is wrong with you? I just finished cleaning and cooking for Ms. Alala. So, your home is next on the to-do-list. What would you like for dinner tonight? I will make a simple avocado club sandwich for lunch and maybe baked fish with rice and peas for dinner. I'll do your laundry and clean the house, so it will take a few hours. You can stay and I'll ignore you or you can go out and do what you came here to do. Dear man, I barely know you but if you wouldn't mind keeping an extra eye on Ms. Alala. I don't like this new version of Mr. Linus."

Ms. Baker watched me very carefully as if she was checking me out. I knew she saw my tears through my sunglasses and just maybe overheard something from my phone call with Aunt Grace. I tried to act normal as I scratched my hair and tried to stretch my arms, diverting her from thinking that I was crying. Rather, I wanted to let her think I just woke up and was stretching.

She watched me with the eyes of a very insightful elderly woman as she said, "Can't hide the tears, my boy. It's good I was screaming out here or others too would have heard your crying. One morning, he woke up and kissed me on my head, hugged me, and asked me to take care of Ms. Alala until he came back with his Ma and his aunt and his best friend, his twin brother from a different mother, Lysandros. He had left for his travel in the morning but returned in a few hours with a completely different personality. It was like he was a different man, very cruel and harsh with Ms. Alala. I won't speak of this to anyone, but I will be here for you and Ms. Alala."

Ms. Baker was glancing at different directions as if she was trying to see if Linus was watching or coming. She shivered in the very sunny and warm day. Her long brown hair was braided up in a bun. Her face was pale white, and her eyes were green like the green grass had painted her eyes from its own palette of colors. Her nose had freckles. She looked like she was around seventy years old. Everyone on the island loved her and allowed her to do as she wished. I wanted to hug her as I realized she was the only woman on this Earth who felt my pain as she too felt it.

She then said, "He somehow changed, and a very different egoistic man came in his place. Now, he is very mean toward everyone. He never glances at anyone directly and wears those goggles even at night. Never before did Mr. Linus ever wear goggles at night or in the rain or shy away from looking into another person's eyes. Please be safe and take care of Ms. Alala and her unborn child as I fear for them. This island feels creepy now as I never felt like this ever before. I came here from the main island when Mr. Linus hired me and my family for the island. I want to actually go back home now that Mr. Linus has left."

I missed Linus so much. I felt like just walking to him and giving him a shake so maybe he would just wake up. I missed talking to him without any worry and just having that friend who was there like the wall whom I could lean on. Yet I had to hold in my feelings, and I would for you, my buddy. As you, my dear friend, had told me, I needed to learn to be patient. This island would give me both patience and the ability to take everything in. I only bought this island on your advice as you had said you felt like it was your destiny. You wanted to be closer to our fathers, yet you never said you would join them without me. You cheated Linus, and that's not fair.

I gave Ms. Baker my keys and gave her a hug. She smiled and hugged me back.

She then suddenly said, "You look like you just walked out of a gothic novel with your black hair and dark brown eyes, that does not match your fair skin. I wonder where you got that face from. Your buddy Mr. Linus, my boy, had shown me your mother and his mother's pictures. They both have brown hair and brown eyes with fair skin, not like Mr. Linus who had beautiful blue eyes, blond hair, and fair tanned skin. Yet I must say never have I seen this Mr. Linus's eyes. Once he was screaming and I thought his eyes had no color but was black. It's not him. I knew it even before I heard your conversation. I promise I will wait for your mother to come and then decide if I should relocate or what. Now my boy, smile and let all the pain be washed away with those wonderful smiles. I promise it helps."

She made me laugh as I knew she was talking out of fear. I was worried why the guy was pretending to be Linus. Ms. Baker then walked on toward my house as I saw she started to tidy up the front porch first. I knew luxury and how the rich live as I am an example of a rich and some say spoiled man. My mother, however, would say I was brought up as a kind gentle man who valued life and didn't take anything in life for granted. I felt like Ms. Baker had so much in common with my mother. Maybe Mum would enjoy her company.

I loved knowing a kindhearted woman cared for the people she worked for and didn't have to worry but did. Humanity was found on this haunted island. She helped me not only for money, but she loved it, and I loved having her here. I missed my mother as even with all the money on this Earth, she always cooked, cleaned, and loved gardening by herself. She had Linus and me do everything with her. We both enjoyed being with her. It was our personal time together as a family, Linus, me, Aunt Grace, and Mum. Our family now would learn to live without Linus. The thought ripped my heart apart, yet I was still breathing and my heart that was beating knew Linus's heart beats no more.

I walked with a heavy heart toward Alala's home. I wondered if I could call Aunt Grace and tell her she was mistaken as Linus was still alive. He was here with me on the Dead Queen's Island. My hands froze as I remembered how he said words that sounded strange to me like maiden and Mummy, and how he warned me to not call his mother. How could he forget his own mother's name and not know his mother, my mother, and we both lived in the same house? We were from the moment of our births, one family under one roof.

Our family had two sisters and their two sons. We always had two floors in our home as one floor was for my mother, and the other floor was for Aunt Grace. Each floor had our fathers' portraits and wedding pictures of each parent displayed as if our fathers were always there. Even at the dinner table, we had always kept two empty chairs for our fathers. Our mothers believed they would unite with their husbands after death and in another lifetime if they only waited and believed in reincarnation.

I saw Alala walking on her front porch. She was breathing hard as if in pain.

I rushed in and asked her, "Are you all right? Where is your husband? Did you call the doctor on the island? I know we have a doctor here on the island. What is it? Why do you seem hurt and are in pain? I have called for my company's doctor to come here. As soon as they can bring her in, she will come."

A very fragile woman stood in front of me, ready to have her kid at any time. Her fingers looked a little swollen as I worried what was going on. Her brown hair fell below her shoulders and above her waist. She had a lot of sunburn from being on the island. She was exercising her feet as they too looked swollen.

Alala smiled and said, "It's not time yet. I still have a few weeks to go. I just get tired and restless at times. I was thinking maybe I should go back to Tasmania and give birth there. My parents are there, and I have never met but know Linus's mother is there too, as is your mother. We spoke during the wedding and a few times on the phone. Your mother called me her daughter as Linus's mother said daughter-in-law. He used to talk about them a lot, eight months ago when I first got pregnant. We so much wanted to surprise you, his mother, and your mother, we didn't realize where time flew by. For almost eight months now, Linus has been acting weird. He had wanted to go and bring his mother and yours. Remember, he came back the same day but has been so different."

Alala touched her belly and sat down on the porch swing. Her curly brown hair blew in the wind as I thought she looked like the most innocent woman on Earth. Her white midi dress came below her knees, and her white sandals exposed her unpainted nails. She had some freckles on her nose which reminded me of my mother who too had freckles on her nose.

Alala was in her own world as she said, "I love Linus so much. We believe we are twin flames born from the same phoenix, separated in life to be individuals, yet got together as we married and will separate at death to reunite again. I will never give up on him even if he acts different. I love him from my inner soul."

She sat and was breathing harder. It seemed like she was having breathing problems. I wondered if that was because her twin flame was not breathing anymore. The thought again split my heart apart.

Alala very quietly said, "When I found out about my pregnancy, Linus was so happy. He wanted to go and bring his mother, Aunt Valery, and you to the island. He went on a trip, but he returned the same night. He left in the morning and returned right after sunset completely changed. He doesn't talk about his mother, your mother, their adventures together, or anything. He never talked about his trip or where he had been for a day or how he came back so quickly. I never asked him. I'll wait for him to say what's going on. We promised we would never lie and always be honest with one another. We also promised to wait for the other person to say what's in their mind before we question them. So, I wait patiently."

Alala got up and tried to walk slowly. I kept standing by her, leaning on the porch railing. I didn't want to look at her directly as it hurt too much to even think my Linus's pregnant wife had been dealing with all this all by herself. Not anymore Linus for I would be with her.

She then said, "We were going to go to your mother's house before the childbirth. All he does now is watch that castle like an obsession. Do you know he never sleeps at night? He never touched me since his return from that one day's travel. Linus said he is too scared to even touch me. He worries he might hurt the baby by accident. Strange, but it's sweet, I think. I do worry where he goes at night. Every night, he walks toward the ocean and then he disappears. I'm so worried if he changed because I got pregnant right after our wedding."

The wind was getting rough as we sat on the porch. I thought about how I saw him in my house last night. He entered without making any sounds. I kept the details from

Alala because I didn't want her to be frightened or be in any danger by knowing anything she wasn't supposed to know. I must keep my friend's wife and his child safe at any cost.

Alala kept changing her position. Once she was standing, then sitting down, and then walking again. It was obvious she was in pain, but she didn't like sharing her pain with anyone. I assumed she thought it would make her seem weak. I knew she needed her husband at this moment, but I knew Linus was so far away. Even if he tried with all his might, he wouldn't make it back.

Alala said, "He walks at night. I think he tries to keep an eye out for everyone on the island. He is so scared of that woman in the castle. I don't fear her, nor do I accept her as any queen of mine. She is dead, so why fear the dead? I feel sorry for her. She is trying to find her twin flame, so she calls for him. She never harmed anyone on the island, so why is Linus so obsessed about her? For the past few weeks, all he does is talk about the Dead Queen. At times, she holds the crown in her hands not on her head, screaming the crown is her husband's. I don't think that's true through. Who knows as their love story has been buried for a thousand years."

I hugged Alala and reassured her everything would be just all right. I heard about the castle and my heart ached for someone even though I had no clue who she was. I wondered why I was pulled toward her. Her love story being buried for a thousand years had me buried within it too. Was she a mermaid who whispers love songs and pulls all me toward her or all other males too? I felt like a cold shiver just ran down my neck.

Then I heard the Dead Queen say, “Beloved, how could you think of me like that? I have been waiting for you and only you for a thousand years. Come to me and let this waiting period be over. I just want to hide in your chest and let no one see me ever again. I can’t see anything until you enter our home again for only then will my sight return. Oh, my darling, I don’t want to see you in a mirror or a portrait but in your complete human form. Give me all the sin you so want but don’t ever give me that one, as my mind, my body, and soul only belong to one and that’s you.”

I was shaking as I knew these words were only for me. I prayed no one else heard them. Yet I saw the shocking look on Alala’s face and knew she heard the words too.

All Alala said was, “Ignore her and try not to invite her to your home. Let’s hope she is buried under the ocean. My mother had said ghosts can only enter if they are invited in. I don’t invite anyone into my house other than my husband. He had knocked after sunset on the day he had left for his adventure across the ocean. He returned home and asked, 'Permission to enter?' I saw it was Linus and I said, 'Always!' The strangest part of this whole phrase was why would he even ask for permission to enter his own home? We rent it from you, but it's our home. It bothers me so much. Why did he need an invitation to enter?"

I was glad he never touched her, but I was worried if he had laid his hands on the baby. I had so many other questions yet said nothing as I saw my company's doctor walk toward us. Alala jolted as her head swirled and her body went forward. She suddenly fainted, but she was extremely lucky someone held on to her and broke the fall until I was able to get to her. There was an invisible hand that held on to her. I swear for a split second I saw Linus holding on to his wife. The tears froze in his eyes when he looked at me.

The doctor who arrived with our ship and crew rushed into the house as I carried Alala to her bedroom. It was then I again saw Linus was hovering over his wife, yet a see-through figure of Linus. He looked at me directly and somehow pleaded to help his wife and child. I was crying in shock. How did Linus show up when his wife really needed him? The telepathy of twin flames was real.

The doctor introduced herself as she said, "I am the doctor your company hired. My name is Geeta Shrivastava.

I was sent by your mother in a private helicopter to personally be here and take care of the people and their necessities. I send anyone with serious health conditions to the mainland. Please give me some privacy as I need to examine her carefully. Maybe you can help me send her to the mainland. She has been anxious for a while. I have spoken to your mother and her mother-in-law. They both advised me not to say anything to her about anything you may know. I'm assuming you know."

It was then the fake Linus walked in and said nothing. He ran toward his wife, but when he touched her, she screamed in pain. I saw the see-through Linus tried to intervene as he threw things at the fake Linus. Geeta jumped up, and I saw the fear in her eyes. She too glanced toward the see-through Linus.

She spoke very clearly without any fear as she told the fake Linus, "Please stay away. She invited you in here but not to touch her. Like I told you and will repeat again, her in-laws hired me because on top of being a medical doctor, I am a seer. I know everyone where you come from knows Theunis Peters, a son of the Kasteel Vrederic. He is very famous in your world. I have worked with Dr. Jacobus Vrederic van Phillip and the Kasteel Vrederic household.

They have sent me with a message to give you. Beware as your time is limited. Everything that begins shall also end."

She stopped and watched the fake Linus. I too knew the Kasteel Vrederic and its inhabitants. The very famous paranormal family is feared in the ghostly world as they are loved in this world. Dr. Jacobus is the most famous doctor of all doctors and the best possible physician around the globe. I realized they had sent Geeta as my mother must have asked for their intervention.

Geeta told the fake Linus, "I don't want you touching her. Her blood pressure is very high, and she needs medical help. I don't know why you haven't sent her to a hospital in Tasmania. Her life and the child's life depend on it. I would want the rich businessman who now owns the whole island, as it's a private island completely run through his family, to help her. You have no say in this matter as now it's in his hands. I can prove you have no say in this matter and so it's good for you to stay out of this matter."

She had an Om symbol on her wrist. I watched Linus move backward as Geeta kept touching her Om bracelet. The bracelet on Alala's hand had a cross symbol, and her wedding band had a cross symbol on the side of it. I realized Aunt Grace had made these wedding bands for both Linus's wife, and my wife. When they would come, they would always be protected. Every time Linus walked closer to her, he moved backward when he touched her. He walked outside and said he would wait there. I knew Geeta had placed the cross-wedding band on Alala's hands as it was not on her hand yesterday.

I saw Geeta as she said, "Her ring was too tight as she gained weight because of her pregnancy. Her mother-in-law had it readjusted and sent it back. I don't know what's going on, but I wouldn't like being here at night. That castle has something going on inside of it. The building is scaring everyone out of their minds."

Linus laughed and said something under his breath. I followed him to the front porch. A crowd had gathered in the front of the house as everyone loved Linus and Alala. I wondered what happened in the last two days. Linus or whoever he was seemed fine just the day before, but he changed. Maybe my arrival changed everything on the island.

Yes, this is my family's private island, completely financed by my family. However, my Linus knew everything that was mine was his too. I would never have it any other way. Linus chose to be here as a schoolteacher so he could be closer to where our fathers had died. He could run our company from anywhere.

I asked Linus, "Where do all the people come from? Every time something or another happens, we have an audience. Is this normal for the island? And where were you last night? Your very pregnant wife was all alone. Do you understand you seem weird and are acting weird? Who are you? Where is my buddy? What have you done with him?"

A black bird flew over us. Linus didn't reply but he looked worried. I saw there were two burn marks on his hands. One was from the cross and the other from the Om symbol. I wondered how and why he had them. He kept looking at the burn marks and I realized he wasn't worried for his wife but rather how he could hide the burn marks. When I first came, they were holding hands and seemed so much in love. How was that possible? Was he changing or did I misjudge them before? How was it that my arrival had changed what he was able to do or what he was not able to do.

He said, "That Indian woman thinks she owns the world. How dare she tells me not to touch my own wife. Who does she think she is? A goddess or something. Does she think I'm the prince of darkness, and she is an Indian goddess? Who then is the singing maiden, the Dead Queen? We all know she haunts the castle, the island, and anyone who goes near the castle. We all should just burn that building. Don't go there, but if you do, then take me along. Alala never wore that cross until today, I don't like any jewelry because I have allergic reactions. These marks are nothing but allergic reactions to any kind of jewelry."

I listened to him and didn't respond as my buddy Linus always had all types of jewelry on him. He would wear a gold cross necklace and had a gold Om bracelet on his wrist. I walked toward the door as I saw Geeta watch him and walk outside. She stood in the open air as she gave Linus a look and didn't even converse with him. She kept the Om symbol close to her chest. Her hands were steady even though I could somehow sense her fear.

She looked toward me and said, "Alala is doing much better, but she needs to be taken to the hospital. I know the babies are in breech position. She has twins and must be operated upon soon. If she faints like this, she will lose both babies and her life. There will be not one but three deaths if we don't rush."

Geeta watched me and gestured with her eyes, but I didn't understand. I didn't know how to tell her I'm not good at signaling or understanding nonverbal cues. The sun high up within the skies was heating up everything around us. I imagined how nice the water would feel. Just to take a dip in the ocean would be amazing. My mind traveled places at the time I needed my mind to be clear and not think of anything but pay attention. I sat on the lounge chair and sunbathed for a while as I waited for Geeta to do her job. Linus walked toward me and sat next to my chair.

He touched my shoulder as I screamed, "Don't touch Aarna, my Maharani, ever again! If you do, I will make sure you regret it. I will haunt you down in this life and beneath the grounds! I will be your worst nightmare! Alive or dead, I will fight till my last breath and will be reborn repeatedly to avenge what was wronged. You hear me you demonic fool, I'm blessed with God's grace. You are cursed, and you can't escape God's punishment even if you have tried for a thousand years."

I don't know what I said or why. Maybe the heat was making me delirious. My mother had said I had no evil bones in my body, but maybe I did in my mind. I touched my own cross and my Om symbol my mother had given me as a child. I had to shake off the weird feelings and thoughts about Linus not being Linus. He had invited me to come here. Linus smiled and watched me intensely. He removed his hand from behind my neck and walked past me to Alala. He touched her belly and was somehow massaging her belly.

As Alala tried to see what was going on, she screamed, "Oh my God! My skin is burning up wherever you, my husband, try to touch me. Ever since your return you never came near me as you burn me every time you lay your hands on me. Even when we sit next to each other, your body is either burning up or freezing cold. Maybe you should get checked to see if you have some kind of island fever. Yes, that's it, you probably have a high fever, associated with some kind of weird virus."

Geeta went to Alala and took her temperature and said, "She is burning up! The places you touched with your hands are burning up even more. What did you do? Let me check you and see if you have a fever, Alala. Maybe I should check you too Linus. I wonder if you have picked up something."

After many hours, the doctor left. Alala was medevacked to a hospital near her parents' house. I called my mother and asked her if she could take care of Alala because her parents were traveling. We couldn't get in touch with them. Linus went with her and somehow whispered something into her ears. I couldn't hear but the young woman looked petrified at whatever he told her.

I was trying to help Alala but in front of me were two Linuses. One flesh and blood or so seemed to be, the other was completely see-through like a ghost, watching over his not ghost but physical wife.

Ghost Linus with his cold icy breath pierced words into my ears as he said, "Sorry buddy for the frozen treatment. I have no other choice. I still love you my twin brother and will always. I don't know who he is, but he murdered me and will probably try to murder my family. Please help me and Alala. Don't tell him you are onto him. I will stay around to help as I believe my God answered my prayers and your prayers combined, as who says prayers are not answered? Remember, the imposter can't see or hear me."

My eyes started to betray me as I watched Linus blow and dry them in place. The air was very humid. It was muggy, sticky, and heavy. The hot day felt even hotter I assumed because of a very negative energy that crawled upon us. I kept an eye on the fake Linus. That's when I saw his face was very strange. He smiled wickedly at me while boarding the helicopter.

He had said in a whisper, so only I could hear, "I assume you know who I am, or maybe you don't yet, either way, it was I who had invited you and your stupid foolish friend here. I played on his weakness as I had murdered both your fathers so I could trap both of you here. So, out of human weakness you two would willingly jump like a leaping frog and return to this island easily. I really needed you just to be here. I needed an invitation to the castle. Glad you have returned the favor, so I can enter your castle easily, or should I say, the Dead Queen's Castle liberally, as I have received an open invitation."

OPEN INVITATION

Moon's
Glowing light
Guides all
Out of darkness,
Warning
One and all
To keep an eye out
For danger looms
All around.
The glowing lantern
Shows
Known and unknown images,
Again, forewarning all
To not invite
The thunderstorm,
The ravishing winds,
Or
The ghostly figures.
So, beware
One and all
Who ask,
Seek,
Or knock

To enter your haven
As the prowlers
Of the dark
Need an open invitation
As they wait,
Bait,
And jump
At the
Unpremeditated
OPEN INVITATION.

Chapter Three:

The Rising Phoenix

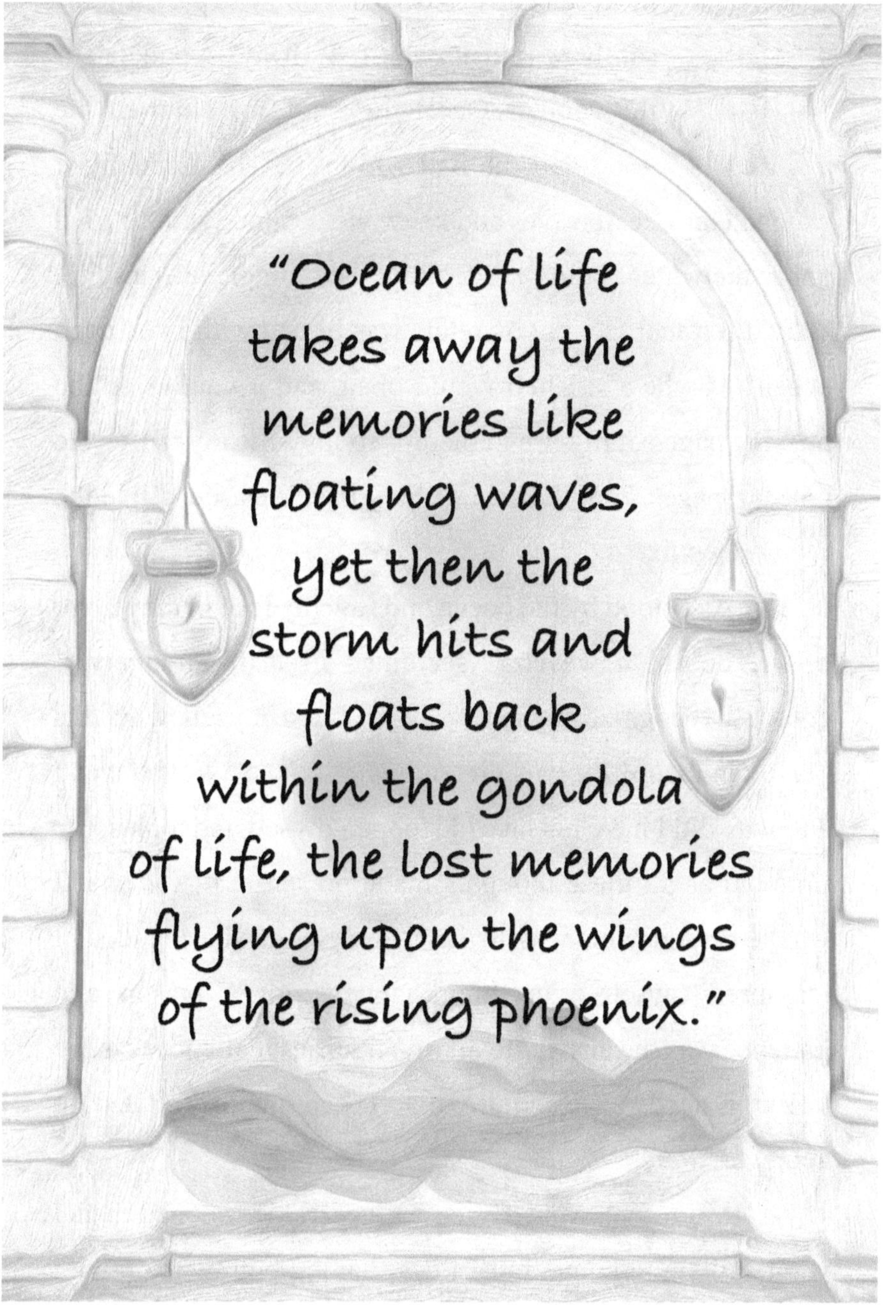

"Ocean of life
takes away the
memories like
floating waves,
yet then the
storm hits and
floats back
within the gondola
of life, the lost memories
flying upon the wings
of the rising phoenix."

The ocean carries the ashes of the departed souls safely within its chest. I always wondered if the Mother Ocean held all her children the good and the bad within her chest equally. I watched the ocean waves and knew the departed souls buried under the water couldn't talk about their simple tales of life. Why did it feel like my own tale was buried within the deep ocean? Maybe a seashell would open, and I would find the missing pages of my life in there. I could write my tale as the missing pages from the ashes of my past life ascend like the rising phoenix.

As I stood by the ocean and saw my face in the mirror of the ocean, however, I screamed in fear. Strangely, I couldn't recognize my own self. I asked myself why this person in the mirror was pretending to be me. Or who was I and why did I have his face? I stopped myself and took some time out as all these thoughts made no sense. It was as if I was a person who was to be feared or maybe dreaded. I reassured myself everything happens for a reason and patience was the answer to all my inquiries. Patience was the virtue I needed to acquire that I had majorly failed to achieve.

Mum and Aunt Grace arrived rather sooner than I wanted them to come, but I loved having both women with me as they felt like the only warm shrug I needed. Geeta came back to the island with them. It had been over a week since Alala left the island with the fake Linus. She had the babies and passed away while giving birth. Her death felt like a pierce in my heart from the beyond. It was reported she had numerous burn marks on her physical body. Her parents were not found as if they too vanished from bottom of the Earth. I had an inkling and knew exactly who might have been involved in this mystery.

Alala's grandmother had cremated her and given her ashes to Aunt Grace to be dispersed into the ocean with her husband. The Linus that accompanied Alala was never found even as the helicopter landed. No one ever saw or heard of him during the births and the whole ordeal. I saw him get on the helicopter, but how and when did he get off? How could he have escaped from the air without anyone noticing?

The pilot told me over the phone, "No sir, there was only the patient and the medical crew members. No other man boarded the helicopter. The patient was unconscious during the whole ride and never regained her consciousness. She was very lucky she had Dr. Geeta with her. Dr. Geeta is one of the best doctors who studied and was supervised by the famous Dr. Jacobus Vrederic van Phillip. That's the only reason the babies are completely normal and alive."

I blamed myself for not being able to protect her or Linus. I was so upset at my ship's captain because he too somehow was missing. He called me and said he would send a relief captain with the crew members. Everything was turning out to be a nightmare rather than a sweet dream I could wake up from. This nightmare continued, as all the things I feared were being piled up on the plate for me.

Geeta stood next to me and said, "I saw Linus enter the helicopter and go with Alala. All the islanders also saw him. Where in the air did he get off? How is it no one knows where he is? I was on the helicopter with Alala when suddenly he was nowhere to be found. All the inhabitants of this island, the ones who work for your family and the ones who were here before your family purchased this island, are scared of that castle. They all want to leave. The Dead Queen of the castle has awakened and is doing all of this. I believe everything is like a mirage of some kind. Sometimes it's just better to let go and start over. We all need to leave and do it quickly."

The islanders were all confused with what was going on. Everyone witnessed Linus getting on the helicopter, yet Mum and Aunt Grace brought his ashes and Alala's ashes with them. Their last wish was for their ashes to be spread within the ocean they loved and wanted to live by forever with each other and their children. It was their plan to save the ashes until both die and then spread the ashes together. They got their last wish as they lived, loved, and died close to one another.

Suddenly from the fog came out a figurine, all dressed in her famous black silk gown. It had lace handsewn on it. The side of the gown had a slit, showing her leg a bit. The gown was very modest and so attractive. She wore jewelry all over her hands, and her crown glowed with nine moonstones on her head. Her hair was laid flat on her back, falling beneath her knees. She had small blue flowers braided on her hair that were forget-me-nots. She had a smell that radiated from her to the whole island which smelled like the sweet-smelling lilacs.

We all saw the Dead Queen of the castle floating on top of the seawall that protects the castle from flooding. She was running in fear, as if her world just turned upside down. I wondered what she feared after being dead for a thousand years. Yes, I was being obnoxious, but I lost two of my best friends and here she was crying, screaming, and running.

She screamed at the top of her lungs, "I am scared! He has returned! Oh my God, where is he? Where are you, my beloved? Why is it I have not been reborn, and he has even after his committed sins? My sins are punishing me, and I do not even know what sins I committed to be punished like this. How is this fair? Answer my prayers, my God, and have mercy. Please let me know how I have wronged if everyone else had wronged me. Please come back to me my beloved and help me. I have been waiting for you for so long. Please do not let go of me and end our love story eternally. Our promises and the eternal love we tied in a knot will be burned to ashes and not rise like the rising phoenix if you let go."

The wind started to blow from all directions. The skies sparked lightning bolts on a clear day. High waves crashed onto the shore as the Dead Queen wearing a black widow's gown cried and shrieked. The woman looked directly at me, and she froze. She was floating backward, and she seemed petrified by my sight. The islanders all looked at her and back at me as they all screamed and ran all over the place. I thought she was blind but then how did she see me?

Everyone forgot about Linus and Alala. I had within my hands the ashes of both in two different urns. I stood my ground as one thing I fought for all my life was justice for all. I would not let a ghost Dead Queen rule my life or dictate to me who she is or who I am. My mother came closer to me as did Aunt Grace. I wouldn't drop or let go of my best friend and his wife. I was going to perform their last rites, so I prayed to my God for intervention.

Aunt Grace said, "Lysandros, listen to me and remember, all the visions of that woman and everything else that is going on are illusions. Don't believe what you see and then they won't be there anymore. Let's perform Linus's last wishes. Remember, twin flames don't separate in life or death. Love keeps them united. They see and believe in one another. Look how both my Linus and Alala proved they are twin flames in life and in death. Believe in only good and good shall come. My child, call upon the good deeds, forgive the ones who have wronged you, and remember at all times, it's not about who wronged you, but that you don't wrong anyone."

Aunt Grace and my mother looked tired and older than they were. I didn't know how the two women were so brave and handling this so honorably. I wanted both women to go back home and not deal with any of this. Yet I had to allow them their right to deal with this their own way. The wind blew my mother's shawl as I saw Aunt Grace wrap it around her. Like sisters they lived their whole lives with the two of us. They forgot the pain of losing their husbands at such an early age, but they were able to go on just holding on to us.

Linus and Alala wanted to go together, not as individuals. They wanted to awaken as individuals but be united as twin flames. They believed they were not whole individually but whole in union. So, with sweet musical notes playing in the back, we scattered their ashes.

Suddenly, I felt a sharp stab puncture my heart. I thought my inner heart was ripped open. My best friend was my last bridge to all the laughs, jokes, and love of my life up to now. The realization hit me strong, I would never see my friend ever again. How would I go on without you Linus? For the first time in my life, I let the tears roll out from my eyes. I wondered how much more teardrops my eyes could hold. My eyes were overfilled, and my teardrops were splashing out freely.

The instrumental music playing in the back became soft and harmonious as we all saw in front of our eyes, two halves of a phoenix rose and became one. It rose from the ocean where Aunt Grace and I had scattered the ashes. The huge phoenix with different shades of colors like red, gold, and purple kept rising. There was a halo around the huge magical bird. Maybe it borrowed the colors and glow from the glowing sun's embers. The magical creature watched all of us, flying toward the Heavenly skies. As our music stopped, we all heard a melodious cry like a musical note come from the phoenix as it showed all its powerful embers.

I thought the magical phoenix nodded its head as I heard Linus and Alala say in union, "Lysandros, we have united and are together. Please take care of our twin girls and give them a loving home with you. Keep them within your chest and care. We pray you and your twin flame unite and rise again in life after life only for one another. Never fear as we will always be near when you need us. Kiss the girls for us as you are all they have. They are yours."

Before the phoenix flew away, in front of all our eyes, radiating gold, orange, and yellow embers fell from Linus's wing down onto the praying palms of my hands. The embers were cool to the touch. As I held them within my hands, I promised to keep them within the safety of my soul eternally. I realized human life might be temporary but love and miracles are eternal.

Just like its arrival, the miraculous phoenix flew away with its vibrant wings spread out as there was still a halo all around it. Then, like nothing had ever happened, everything disappeared. As everyone was talking about what we had just seen, a crying shrieking woman's voice shattered the whole island like we didn't have enough for the day.

She screamed with a painful cry, "Oh God, it is not fair. Everyone dies and reincarnates with their beloved by their sides. I have been praying to You for a thousand years. Yet my beloved still does not appear. Why have I been punished? Why am I feared as I know and fear, he is back. Tell me God, are You not my Creator? Am I not Your creation? Then why is there a different standard for me? Why have I then been judged unjustly? Someone, please help me! Oh my God, I will never stop believing in You. Even if You do not love me, I still love You. Maybe my sin is I love him too much, more than my living breath. I will die for him over and over again."

Finally, there was silence. The islanders witnessing this phenomenon started talking amongst themselves. They were saying they all had enough and would be leaving the island. The sun was setting in the vast skies as I walked away from the crowd, over to the dock. My ship had just arrived as did the new captain sent by my good old trusty captain. The new crew members including the renovation team for my newly purchased castle also arrived.

Mum and Aunt Grace refused to stay after the funeral through the night. They had a different ship ready and insisted on taking the girls back home with them until I figured out what to do with the island. Tears ruled everything around us, as fear and the questions of why, how, and for what overpowered any mind of understanding. Everyone agreed to the terms of the girls being with Mum and Aunt Grace until everything here settled down.

I hugged and kissed my two baby girls, telling them, "This godfather of yours will forever hold you two within my chest. For now, you two will be safe with your grandmother and grandaunt."

My mother said as she was ready to board the ship, "Lysandros, please forget everything and come with us. I am frightened by all this and would stay with you, but I can't risk the babies of Alala and Linus. They are now our responsibility and blessings. I feel like I should take them as far away as I can to keep them safe. I never liked this island and again don't like it. It has taken away so much and those I loved one by one."

I hugged my mother and Aunt Grace. I had to get them and the babies off this island. I took some of the ash I saved from the embers I received from their father Linus and drew crosses on their chest. In front of my eyes, I watched the crosses turn into an amber color and were placed within a crown. I knew that must have been a symbol of protection for my two beloved girls as a blessing from their father.

I told them all, "I will come, but as you both know I must find out what happened to my friend. The only way of finding out is for me to finish the Dead Queen's story."

I bid them farewell with my ship's captain who was standing with me. Dirk van Schipper, an old friend, had volunteered to help my family, whenever we needed his help. He came to the island because I assumed my mother spilled all the beans to him. Dirk, Linus, and I were buddies from early childhood. I hugged Captain Schipper, or as I call him by his first name, Dirk.

Dirk hugged me back, saying, "I came to be with you, so I brought two ships. I brought the big one and a small emergency one with two extra captains, so one can take Aunt Valery, Aunt Grace, and the girls back. We can keep the small emergency one if we need it. The two other captains can go back and forth taking anyone who wants to return to the mainland. Let's get this haunted island figured out. I want to get to the bottom of this story without being told to go to the bottom of the ocean. Hey, think about it. We didn't have to sneak out and go to the movies. Also, I don't think Linus would have liked it if we kept him out. So, he wanted to be the center of attention. Oh boy Linus, you still win from wherever you have gone to."

I thought about what Dirk said and I could see the three of us as young boys sneaking out to go to the movies. Mum found out each time, but Dirk had gone home to sleep without any guilt. Linus and I would spill the beans as we were scared all night thinking about horror figures climbing in through the windows. The memory gave me a good feeling as I knew I had those memories with me forever.

Dirk was laughing as he said, "Linus will come back, somehow. He will sneak back in. I am telling you, just mark my words. Until then we have our memories. Okay Linus, when you do come back, let me know what I have won."

Geeta saw all of us and began crying for her patient whom she tried to save with everything she could. The wild winds came from nowhere as Geeta's black hair flew all over and blocked Dirk's view.

She wiped her eyes with her hands, whimpered, and very quietly said, "Sorry everyone. I'm trying to separate the doctor patient part. Somehow this time, it's harder. When I was treating Alala who I knew was in trouble, Aunt Valery and Aunt Grace were depending on me. I didn't like the evil Linus lookalike from the get-go. There was something fishy about him and I should have trusted my gut feeling."

Geeta stopped and took her sandals off as there was sand in them. She was wearing a white dress with hand-embroidered blue forget-me-nots. The sleeves came to her wrist and the dress fell just beyond her knees. Her long black hair was blowing with the wind. She wore small blue pearl drop earrings and a matching necklace. The pearls had the Om symbol drawn on them. On her wrist was a matching bracelet with a huge Om symbol on it.

She surveyed the ocean but again teared up as she put her sandals back on and said, "I tried to warn everyone. What could I have said? I believed Linus was from Mars. He seemed different. I couldn't voice my thoughts, but I wish I had. Lysandros, please let me come with you to the castle. I must see the end of this story. God forbid if any one of you happen to get sick, I want to be there and start treating you before anything happens. I must see the end of this story, even if that means I might not be on Earth to write the end of my own story. I want to be a part of yours. That's my story."

The situation was beyond anyone's imagination. I hugged my mother so hard for the same reason. She asked me if something was wrong. She knew Linus was a part of my whole being. He was like her second son. I didn't know what to say or who to blame. My heart kept saying it couldn't be the Dead Queen. Yet I knew everyone accompanying me to the castle thought it was all her evil doings.

I laughed and said to Geeta, "Some stories don't have endings. They only have beginnings and remain a mystery. Those are the stories people love to read and retell, not the ones with happy endings. Stories with tragic endings are my personal forte. My books with tragic endings are my bestsellers. No, I didn't get rich by selling books. I was born into it as you all know, yet I love to write the tales of a fictional world where I can control the narrative."

Dirk started to laugh as he looked up to the skies. I knew he was talking to Linus. So many nights I watched my buddies secretly read my books, trying to see if I had any kissing in them. They would get bored when they realized I only wrote clean novels that families could read together. My two goddaughters could read all my books, and I would allow them to read novels about their parents when I finish writing the novel I came to the island to write. I blew a kiss to my goddaughters in my head and smiled as I breathed in their scents.

I told Geeta and Dirk, "I never wanted to live in any one of my books as I allowed my characters to have privacy. So, I never actually lived on any island but just visited the different locations. Don't ask how I became the owner of this small island. We were helping people set up a world where they could support themselves and create a world where fairytales could come true."

We all looked up toward the castle on the hill as I said, "Our vision was not to become a part of a horror movie. There are one hundred people employed to live here, their family members, and the original inhabitants. Combined, we have a population of two hundred fifty residents. Yes, Geeta, you can accompany me. Everyone employed or living on the island can come to the castle. My doors are always open to all."

We walked up to the castle. Dirk laughed and hugged everyone in our group. He said nothing but walked past me and stood in the courtyard of the Dead Queen's Castle. He took a deep breath and prayed. We all didn't miss him doing the sign of the cross. It was a ritual we all did as we blessed ourselves and all around us.

Geeta laughed and said to Dirk, "A very nice way of seeing life. I love your attitude. No wonder Aunt Grace insisted you come along on this trip. You pray and you like to live life to the fullest. You have such a positive energy glowing all around you. With the positive way of thinking included within your soul, I believe you will make sure Lysandros is just fine. Oh yes, and all of us, yourself included."

We all laughed. I knew Geeta was a really good doctor and a seer of some kind. I wondered what else did she see in the castle that she would probably never share? I didn't have the courage to ask.

I didn't know how long we were all walking, but it felt like a very long time. We walked from the edge of the ocean to the castle grounds. It felt like a never-ending walk. I didn't realize how far the castle was from my cottage. From my windows, the castle looked like it was next door.

The courtyard was huge. There was a maze of flowering rose bushes that kept the unnerving feeling alive. I've always loved manicured gardens, but this one gave me the creeps. The garden reminded me of burial grounds. The different colored roses didn't calm my nerves, but I didn't voice my feelings. Geeta and Dirk were still praying as we continued to walk. A Hindu and a Christian were praying next to one another as I walked past them.

The roses were all blooming like they had a personal gardener who had been taking care of them. There was not a single dead bud amongst the roses. They were all beautifully pruned. Winter's miraculous roses were blooming reminding us miracles are blessings from the Divine. The evergreen bushes were all cut to perfection. No unkempt bushes, ivies, weeds, not even any fallen leaves were found in the completely fenced two hundred acres of land that belonged to the castle.

Geeta was talking to herself as she said out loud, "If no one has taken care of this property or has ever set foot in here for a thousand years, then who planted these plantings? Where did all the flowers come from? To my knowledge, roses weren't introduced to this area until more recently. So, who is taking care of them? It can't be the Dead Queen. Okay, that thought gives me the creeps. How did all of these survive for a thousand years? As an Indian, I don't know why you call yourself Maharani, like great queen translated to English. I call you the Dead Queen."

We continued walking through the courtyard. I saw shiny green pinnate leaves and reddish flowers on a bush. I immediately knew I wrote about this endangered plant in one of my books. King's Lomatia, also called Lomatia Tasmanica, could be one of the oldest plants in the world at roughly about 43,000 years old. How did an unkept ghostly castle have this plant? I laughed to myself with realization that a ghostly castle would have it.

Geeta came near me and whispered in my ears, "How well do you know this captain? He seems weird and gives me the chills. He reminds me of someone, but I can't place my mind to it. Why is he laughing when we are all dying in fear?"

I laughed and thought to myself, why would she ask such a weird question? But then again, after fake Linus, I don't even trust myself. Should I tell her my regular captain quit because he was having marital problems, so one of my two best friends volunteered? Maybe because we both lost one out of three, we both wanted to make sure we didn't lose one another. Two ships came, one with my mother, Aunt Grace, and our personal staff. The other one came with some of my employees I requested to have. I do know all of them.

Dirk had sunglasses on even on a very dark and gloomy day. All my ship captains tend to wear sunglasses, yet I knew my friend was a crier, so he would wear his glasses to hide the tears he didn't want anyone to see. I decided not to say anything to Geeta as some things were very personal and she would have to figure out on her own.

The castle door opened. My cook, cleaners, gardeners, driver, security, and the manager of all my employees walked in behind us. I felt a bolt of lightning inside of my chest. There was a crown that was so familiar circling above my head like a vortex, pulling me into a tunnel. I had the drowning sensation even during my awakening state. There was an ocean where I saw myself drowning and I couldn't ask for help because my mouth was taped.

The warm hands of Geeta broke my awakening nightmare. I assured her I was fine. I saw her worried face. Maybe she was a mind reader. Or maybe a seer can see things we the normal people couldn't see.

Geeta yelped in a loud voice, "Captain Schipper, don't walk so close to me please. You scare me and I don't trust you. I only trust Lysandros and Aunt Valery and Aunt Grace. I will leave as soon as I can leave the island after making sure you all are safe. This whole island is giving me the creeps."

Geeta began crying as she said, "Dr. Jacobus sent me here so I could avoid a forced marriage my father arranged for me, which I refused. I was going to be sent back to India to marry this strange doctor I have never met. Now I feel like I should just accept and forget any chance of a knight in shining armor coming for my rescue. Even though I feel like I can't breathe in here, I don't want to disappoint Aunt Grace who has always been there for me. I must be here for her son and Alala."

Dirk walked behind me as he took his sunglasses off. He fixed his hair and was either laughing or crying, I couldn't tell. His eyes were red. Linus would laugh and joke how Dirk always cried, even when he was watching an episode of Scooby-Doo. Dirk would jump up in fear or cry because he couldn't have that much food. He cried he couldn't have the food Shaggy had with Scooby. We had a lot of fun growing up together.

Dirk said, "When I get scared, I tend to laugh in hysteria. It's not normal but I do. Lysandros, listen my buddy, I want to share my thought. I'm more scared why Dr. Shrivastava feared me. Can she predict death just by looking at people? Tell her to just let me know if she thinks something is wrong with me. I know she is a seer, so it's like she could see my death. Oh God, just say it."

I saw Dirk's face for the first time as he took off his sunglasses. I thought to myself where did I get this friend from? He was a devoted friend and ship captain, but I worried if he was the right person for this job. I didn't say anything because he was shaking so much in fear that we all heard the floorboards creak from his shaking.

Dirk again bumped into me, and I saw he was wearing a huge cross. He also had a rosary wrapped around his wrist. I wondered if he had the Bible with him. Then, I saw in his pocket he had not one but two copies of the Bible. I could read both my friends because I loved them so much.

He was still shaking, so I held his hands and asked him, "Where on Earth did you come from? Are you my buddy Dirk? I worry if not, then who sent you here and who recommended you for this job? Dirk, just try to relax and remember in this world, you have me. In the other world, Linus is there."

Dirk came and stood next to me in the grand hallway of the castle. He smiled and nodded his head. If he moved even a step more, he would be on my lap. From my knock, he would be flat on the floor. Forget any ghosts, he would have to worry about me.

Dirk knew I was getting annoyed. I didn't have time to babysit anyone on this journey, especially a big, huge baby. I knew I was being annoying as I didn't fear this ghost, Maharani, Aarna, or as all call her the Dead Queen. Yet she was a dead ghost people feared, and they had a right to fear her. Dirk too was in his right to fear this dead Maharani.

Dirk with a very broken voice got some words out as he said, "You know I was born in Naarden, the Netherlands. My family members are family friends of Dr. Jacobus Vrederic van Phillip. For some reason, his family is worried about all of us and this mysterious island. As you know, Aunt Valery is his patient. She called him for help. I can't believe Linus is not here as the three of us always vacationed together. I love vacationing with you my buddy, but this is way scarier than the island vacation I had in mind. Now I'm worried if I will ever get to see my buddy Jacobus again."

I wondered why he was babbling. Jacobus saved not only my mother but also Linus when he had a heart transplant surgery. That was one reason I knew the fake Linus was fake. He had no sign of the heart transplant surgery. I kept all of this in my mind and hoped the Dead Queen couldn't read minds. If Dirk still remembered Jacobus, then he really was my childhood friend Dirk, not another fake like Linus.

How did Jacobus know about this castle, when I did not? He had warned me a long time ago to avoid buying weird islands and castles. Regardless, Captain Schipper was my buddy, Dirk, and he helped my family and me just by being a friend. I wouldn't risk my friend's life. If he wasn't comfortable, then I would make sure he could leave or do as he wished.

Geeta asked Dirk, "Why are you talking about Dr. Jacobus now? He is my guru, and I don't like you taking his name in a haunted castle. For Heaven's sake, if you knew him, how come I do not know you? I was trained by him in the Netherlands. I guess he keeps personal friends and work colleagues separate."

I looked at both as they were both sweating as the castle was so hot. I hoped we wouldn't get to hear much of these two fighting. Why were both of them acting weird? Maybe because of the presence of unnatural forces.

Dirk looked at Geeta and said, "I wanted to make sure my friend knows I'm not fake. I'm his real buddy, Dirk. I'm scaring myself because of Linus. How did Alala not know? Maybe because she loved him so much, she just wanted him by her side at any cost. So, she ignored all the signs."

I ignored them both as I tried to pay attention to my property manager who while giving a tour of the property said with a very annoying voice, "This part of the entry gate to the garden is new. We added this at your suggestion. We tried to match the thousand-year-old antique gate. Workers refused to enter beyond this point, so all of these were added to the original building through a breezeway. The open stone breezeway leads to that huge wooden door which opens to the old castle. Remember, as you start to live here, this property has been updated but is still over a thousand years old."

He seemed annoyed too and I figured out people become different when they are touched by or near any unnatural sources. So, I had to be careful to make sure everyone stays themselves and are not too influenced by any ghost.

The property manager then said to me, "Usually, these properties become uninhabitable as no one has entered the building in a thousand years. If everything falls apart, I hope you have enough insurance to cover everything. You own the island and the castle too, so you can do what you want to with this horrific castle. There are no restrictions from anyone. Maybe you can have a small church or a prayer house here, so the unnatural beings can leave."

Most of the members of my team were refusing to enter the castle. I was shocked no one came forward except for Geeta, Dirk, my business manager Ashok, and myself. There were local workers I hired and paid in advance who too refused to enter. Ashok took upon himself the responsibilities of the renovation to bring the castle up to date.

He said, "I am not afraid of all the rumors related to the castle or the Dead Queen who haunts the island. I actually live within a horror house and a horror queen, my wife, who threatens to leave me every other day. So, this break will test how strong our union is. If it's meant to be, it will last. If it's not, she is welcome to leave."

I knew whatever Ashok said or didn't say, he wouldn't leave without knowing what happened to Linus as he too worked with Linus closely. I didn't care who accompanied me or did not. I knew this was my destiny and I would complete this journey without any fear. My best friend Linus passed away for this cause, and I wouldn't let his death go in vain. I would avenge his death.

Why did the demon take his face? He didn't stop at taking the face of Linus but also murdered my best friend and his wife in cold blood. How did he take their lives so easily? I wanted to find out the truth. I wanted to get to the bottom of this.

We were still walking in the courtyard of the castle which was covered like a mini castle. I opened the main door of the castle with the original golden key I had received at purchase. Suddenly, there was a draft. Cold chilling winds blew out from within the castle onto us. There was a sweet smell which came flowing out that hurt my nose. I felt dizzy and thought everything around me was spinning, like I was in a tunnel.

A crown was circling again, so I was traveling into another vortex. I didn't know if I was steady enough to walk into it. I smelled the ocean, and I felt a cold knife-like piercing ice hit me. A woman's scream ripped the air as I saw half of a phoenix come toward me and scream her lungs out. I presumed she made everyone deaf with it.

That's when I saw a therianthrope, a creature which was a half man and half beast. It's a shape shifter which could live in air, underwater, or on land. The creature came flying in and landed on the balcony. It was the same balcony where the Dead Queen had appeared and had called me and all the islanders for a thousand years.

He flew in and smiled like he enjoyed all this drama he alone was causing. I knew he was demonic as did everyone in our group who dared to enter, and those who eventually followed us in. In front of the beast stood a half phoenix who became the Dead Queen with a blindfold over her eyes. Yet, I could see through the blindfold, instead of normal eyes, she had two black stones.

She wore all black and stood there trying to find her way through. I realized she was blind. Behind her the beast advanced and slowly came near her. His face was strangely familiar, but I knew he was a shape shifter, so I didn't know what he actually looked like.

As he neared the Dead Queen, we saw a beautiful mystical phoenix rise from the ocean by the castle. The phoenix dropped a tear on the beast and in front of my eyes the beast disappeared like burnt smoke. There was a bad smell like something was just burnt or cremated. It made me nauseous as the air felt contaminated.

The beast whispered in the air, "Oh all you living humans, fear me. Fear my words. Fear even my reflection for I am always watching you from behind. I am always one step ahead of you. Hear my words as the Dead Queen will not hear me. Remember dear Aarna, sweetheart of mine, I will be back only for you. I will murder him again to only unite with you. Oh yes, all you foolish ones who have dared to join him, I will have fun plucking you all out one by one, just like I plucked out Linus and his dearly devoted and beloved wife."

I watched the Dead Queen twirl in a circle as she was falling into the ocean. Somehow the powerful demonic beast had hurt the Dead Queen. I wondered how he harmed a dead person. Maybe in their world, they could fight with one another. We all watched her fall into the deep ocean as if she died again. The body of Maharani, the Dead Queen, was then lifted mystically from under the ocean, as the sleepy and lifeless body now slept upon the wings of the rising phoenix.

THE RISING PHOENIX

Under the ocean
Lies the hidden truth
Buried within the dead.
When the body is lifeless,
All the pages
From the diaries of life
Wash away
Like floating candles
In the water of life.
Yet how would the untold,
And the unknown
Love story ever be bound,
I wondered.
I knew the answer,
Through the tears,
The fires,
And from the ashes of
THE RISING PHOENIX.

Chapter Four:

The Bloody Mirror

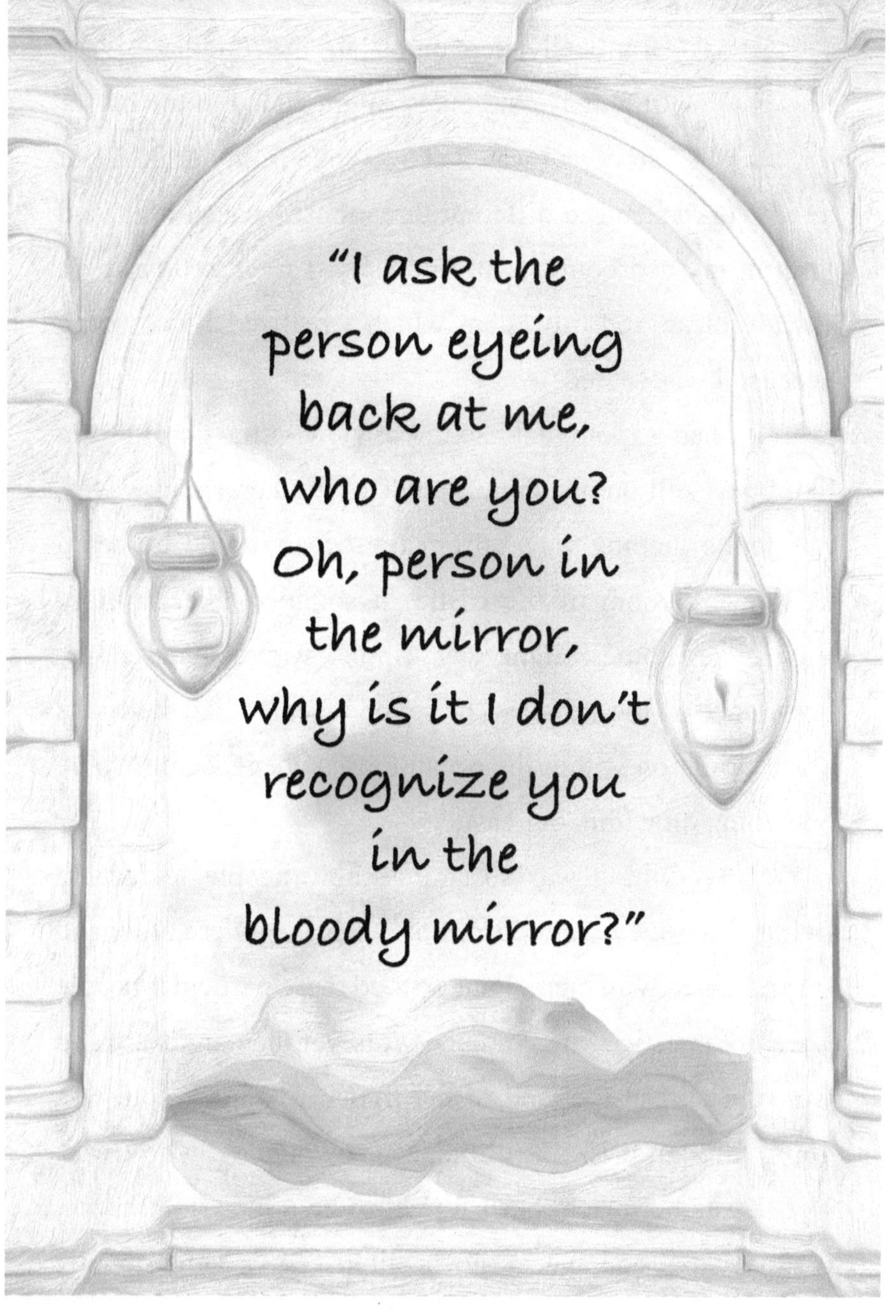
"I ask the
person eyeing
back at me,
who are you?
Oh, person in
the mirror,
why is it I don't
recognize you
in the
bloody mirror?"

The new living members of the castle were all frantically screaming in the middle of the night. The moonless night added to the horror story as I watched everyone from our group of hired workers run in different directions. I paced back and forth in my bedroom absent-mindedly. I tried to tidy up an already clean and tidy room which I realized I was doing because I was scared.

I had a room that had direct view of the ocean. I felt like I was still on my ship. Sounds of loud crashing waves, not gentle lapping waves from the ocean, could be heard from every room of the castle. It sounded like capillary waves, or some might say ripple waves, caused by turbulence on the surface. The sounds seemed like there was a war going on within the ocean too, as there seemed to be one going on within our castle.

Everything was so strange how people feared the living when they were dead, not when they were alive and sat and dined with them. I understood these particular people were not ones we sat and dined with, yet they are dead, and we were still in the land of the living. My inner soul was going through the same turbulence. I wondered who I was. Yes, I was born rich, but I fought to be a man with honor, dignity, and courage. I never linked my name to any negativity and would not until my last breath. I would fight to undo the wrong that had been done here even if that means I must fight with the spiritual world and fight with myself.

The screams of the frightened inhabitants of my home ripped the peace and quiet of the night. I could within all the screams tell apart the screams of Dirk who screamed louder and higher pitched than an opera singer. I told myself this is my home, and I was not a king and not married to anyone be it she was a queen or not. So, I would ask all non-invited people to leave. I didn't want any negative people, dead or alive, in my home.

Dirk needed to stop screaming like this or he could wake up the dead even faster than they can leave. He might with his screams kill the living people or make everyone deaf and would have more ghosts to deal with. I would congratulate him later for increasing the ghost population. I walked outside the door, and I saw Geeta and Dirk run toward the family room. I thought Dirk was screaming in fear as Geeta kept shouting at Dirk to shut up.

Geeta said, "If you don't shut up, I will give you something to shut up. Then, you won't have the chance to run but just become another ghost and increase the ghost population."

I laughed as that's what I was thinking. Dirk didn't shut up as his mouth was still open, but no sounds were coming out of it. I guess he feared Geeta.

The balcony doors were all left ajar. I saw the wall in between the ocean and the house that looked like a brick wall with doors, was completely open. I did not understand what was going on. It seemed like our home and the ocean were becoming one. Or we were in the ocean, although we were not. Everything was just a figment of my imagination. I needed to control myself and give courage to all the others.

Through the open wall, we saw a pair of hands all covered in blood come floating in. The floors were being covered by dripping ocean water piling up in middle of the room like a reflecting pond. Was the water piling up or did a glass floor appear? As the floors were covered in blood, the screams of Dirk and all he infected with his screams were making everyone deaf.

The bloody hands went in all directions, and we all realized they belonged to a woman. One hand reached out toward the front door as it was left open. A very frightened voice of a fragile woman said with terror, "Please help me! I am so scared what is going on. Please help me! He will kill me again."

Her whispers were like intense sound waves. They broke the molecules and literally tore matter apart. Her words shattered the whole castle. Windows and doors were all shattering. I didn't even realize how the wooden castle doors or shutters once ajar made the castle open to the whole village. It's like I could see the whole village just as I had seen the castle from my small cottage. Everyone on the island saw what was happening inside of the castle.

The terrified woman asking for help terrorized all the living breathing beings of the castle. Screams from the castle could be heard all over the island. The islanders were all walking with lanterns and screaming in fear. I felt like my ear drums were shattering from just Dirk screaming. I held him by his long brown hair and placed a finger on his lips, signaling to him to shut up. His head was now nodding as he calmed down. I assumed because everyone else was screaming, he figured he could take a break.

A woman's voice from the village crowd said, "They woke her up. She is back and will haunt down every single one of us. These foreigners must meddle in everything just because they have money. Hey, you rich man, why couldn't you mind your own business and leave us alone? Go back to where you came from. When you leave, remember to burn the castle down."

In the crowd was Ms. Baker as I saw her punch the screaming woman and hold her down with her own body. Ms. Baker was my one-woman army. She punched and shoved all who spoke against us.

Ms. Baker joined the screaming group and said very loudly so everyone could hear, "You leave Lysandros alone. It's because of him you even have a job, a house, and food on your table. You all knew about the evil dead woman. It's time we tell her to leave our island or burn her, not him. He is the reason your family members have food on your table."

Everyone in union was screaming in fear. People say the weirdest things in fear, anger, or sadness. I knew that and would never hold a grudge over frightened people. Suddenly, I saw there amidst everyone was standing the fake Linus. I saw him laugh and join everyone else in a chant. He was trying to intimidate people and get them to declare war with my group and me.

The fake Linus joined the chant and said, "I was gone for a while, and he took over the island. He even convinced everyone I was dead. They scattered the ashes of my wife in the ocean without my permission. Now he is going to trick everyone he is good, and I am bad. Did you ever think, maybe my wife died because she was not my twin flame?

You all killed her as you took her away from this island. I blame you all for my Alala's death."

I saw Linus stand in the middle of the crowd and knew it was not him. My Linus would take the blame honorably and not ruin our friendship. In time, he would explain to me the truth, not by embarrassing me in front of everyone. Numerous times in our short lifetime together, we both honorably took blame for one another. We would take the blame to our death bed. Dirk came and stood by me. He held my hand and gave it a positive squeeze.

Tears poured out of my eyes not in fear or hurt but because my friend's name and face were being used by a demon for reasons not known to me. I stood there and made a promise. My Linus, I would avenge your death, my friend, and that I would do even to my last breath.

Dirk said out loud, "I would give up my life to prove our friend Linus would never do that or be like him. My buddy is an honorable man. He would take all the blame to his death bed, but never would he dishonor us. You're not my buddy Linus. You don't even know who I am, nor do you know where I came from."

That's when we saw a phoenix circle our castle as it poured water on everyone from its wings. The crowd of onlookers started to leave and walk back to their homes. It was like they were all being washed away.

The one woman who had spoken earlier said, "He is the demon. He has a demon bird which he uses to control everyone. Please, try to fight this demon! He is in a human form, but I believe he is a demon."

Some people stopped listening to her, but most of them just left. It was then I saw the woman who was talking became a black crow and she flew above the fake Linus's head. In front of my eyes, he turned into a half-man and half-beast form and disappeared. Behind all of this, we forgot about the hands. As I turned, in front of me were the wet hands dripping with blood. A woman dressed in all black was standing there.

She had a black blindfold over her eyes, and she said, "Dear beloved, I will avenge your death even if that means I must be in purgatory for the rest of my life and must dress in all black as your widow. I will never let other men, rich or famous, touch me. I, the queen of this castle, will always be known as the prisoner's widow, who waited for her beloved husband for a thousand years, only to unite with him."

The whole castle filled up with smoke and a smell came with it. Everyone was having a hard time breathing as

I saw the black widow feared by all disappear. The new inhabitants of my home, not her castle, ran in fear.

The cook said, "Everything I cook turns into dark stingy food. I know she is poisoning us. I will leave, sir, on the next available ship. I don't want to die of fear here. I can't even eat my own cooked meals in fear."

The woman was very tall. Her hair was covered with a cap, and she had an apron on. She had tears in her eyes as she was shaking and trembling in fear. Her lips looked pale, and her face seemed like she was a walking dead person. Geeta stood there watching this poor woman.

I told Geeta, "Please handle her. She can leave on the next ship when it arrives. I don't think anything is coming in two weeks though. So, everyone here is stuck on the island for the next two weeks. Everyone knew what they signed up for and agreed to come on their own. There is free housing, free schooling for children, and an income for all who are employed in the castle or within the island. All they need to do is make the island a paradise for the visitors. So, dead or alive, we must somehow stay here on the island. Anyone who wishes can go to one of the cottages in the village or stay here in the castle."

I walked upstairs through the very old and antique staircase. It was a never-ending circular staircase that felt magical, like it appeared from a magical book, and wouldn't end until you closed your eyes and said please just stop. The wooden steps all made horrific sounds when I stepped on them. I thought each step complained and was saying I was too heavy for them. Or maybe they said, get lost.

Finally, I ended on the upper landing of the staircase. As I stood by the open window, it was then I suddenly felt like I was being sucked into a whirlwind which looked like a crown, or rapidly spinning air. Maybe it was a vortex because as the air was rising rapidly. I was being sucked into it like how a vacuum cleaner sucks in debris. I couldn't stand on my feet, but the pull was so strong I knew I had to just let go and allow the pull to take its course.

A woman wearing a soft pink dress was running through a field of pink flowers. She looked like a part of the flowers, or should I say she was the flower fairy giving something from her soul to make the flowers glow. The image was so mesmerizing I forgot how a few seconds ago my lungs needed air. I felt suffocated yet now my eyes were witnessing the most beautiful woman in the universe run.

She ran into me and said, "You smell like the ocean! When did you come back? What did you bring for me from your trip this time, my love? I missed you and prayed may we never be separated in life or in death. Promise me you won't live or die without me. I believe in reincarnation, and I pray you who does not believe in reincarnation be reincarnated just for me. From high above the skies and down below the ocean or on Mother Earth, may we always unite with one another. I don't ever want to be reincarnated without you."

I stood there without uttering a single word. It was then I was being sucked into another vortex tunnel where again I saw the same woman. She wasn't free and running around like the flower fairy but crying in fear.

She took out a tucked away handkerchief hidden within her bodice and very gently wiped her eyes as she said, "It matters not if I live or die. I will never allow another man to touch me. I do not care if God hates me. How could I tear open my soul and give it to another man? Father, please! I forbid you! Please do not let this happen to me. I am his bride and I carry his child. I will not allow another man to come into my life. I will not allow you or anyone else to touch me or my child. I do not fear death or being in purgatory forever, but I will not allow anyone to break my everlasting bond with my husband."

There were two men standing in front of her. She was dressed all in black as she stood there and defied the two men. She screamed and shouted her lungs out. She tried to scratch them when they tried to touch her.

She cried and prayed as she said, "God, please tell me what to do. They will kill me and my unborn child. Tell me how I could jump out of this window and save my honor, not be raped and killed by them."

There was one man covered from head to toe in weird clothing. He reminded me of Incubus. I thought Incubus always mesmerized people with his looks. This person terrified me with his huge, sharp, exposed teeth, which he clenched while smirking at the same time.

He was hissing like a snake as he said, "You belong to me. We were betrothed to each other as children. I don't accept your secret wedding! I declare you to get rid of that child and marry me within the next two weeks. Otherwise, I will have your head! I will make sure your unborn child never gets to see this world. I do not accept any eternal ties between a man and a woman. We the men just take as many women as we want, or you know at times just need."

The woman in black screamed and shouted at both men. She rubbed her womb and placed her lose hair in a bun.

She then in a cold pitchy piercing voice said, "Father, I had accepted you as my own father. Even though you married my mother and had her impregnated by another man. All my life I assumed she was a hooker, so I hated her. Yet you just showed me you are not my father and never were. All you wanted was this castle as you are trying to get your goon wedded to me. I will not as he is like my stepbrother. I will never marry him, nor will I give this kingdom over to him. I do not believe my husband Lysandros is dead. How could he die if I, his beloved Aarna, the Maharani of this castle, the true Queen of this Kingdom, am still breathing? How could God allow one half of the twin flame to be alive if the other half is dead?"

I was somehow dumped out of the whirlwind. Someone was trying to either kill me or maybe show me something. Either way I was being pulled in and out of a vortex that made me feel like I died and just got back to life. The feeling drained my strength. As I jumped back, I wondered how I could then be her twin flame, or she be mine if I am still in the land of the alive and she was in the land of the dead.

I was wheezing, coughing, and breathless. Medically they would say I was suffering from dyspnea. I told my heartbeats to not stop beating because my beloved's heartbeats had stopped. I needed to find out what happened here. I was going from one place to another. How did I enter the memories of the past? How was all of this happening?

My heart called her name without fearing her, the black widow who haunts the island and is feared by all the residents. Why was it I didn't fear her when everyone else did? I punched my heart and asked myself repeatedly why my heart cried for a dead woman. Why did I feel like something big was lost? Where did I lose the biggest secret of all my rebirths?

I assumed rebirth was a chance for the soul to learn from the past mistakes and equalize karma, so we get another chance in life. How was it fair or possible if we didn't remember what we have done in our past life? How did karma work? Maybe I had it all wrong. Maybe rebirth was actually a cycle, not just a redo of life.

Separated by just one heartbeat my beloved and I were. Yet I promised if we were meant to be together, then I would cross the bridge of life and come to my beloved on the bridge of death. I heard cries of a woman break the silence in my quiet lonely home. The windows and doors were shaking like they would shatter. I still didn't fear even though I saw most of my staff members leave in the middle of the night afraid of her.

The few staff members I had left were all trying to leave. I had employed only a few with so much money. It felt bad, how much money I had been spending for this one castle. I could afford the whole village with the same finances if things were different. We opened all the windows and doors of the castle to let the outside air, voices, and all the sounds in. At any time, we could close the windows and doors to keep the sounds from getting in or out.

I watched my staff members all speak together very loudly so I could hear them, “She is evil. No amount of money will keep us here even for one night. She is dead and has been dead for a thousand years. She must have been bad for God to punish her like that. How could a soul remain in the same place for a thousand years?”

The dark night made everything very horrific like everyone came to live in a fantasy but when reality clicked, we all realized we were all in a haunted castle. So, I couldn’t blame anyone who wanted to just get out of there. I would do the same thing under normal circumstances. Fear could drive people crazy. Why should I not let their fear talk when they were all just afraid of a one-thousand-year-old dead woman?

Why didn’t she scare me? Instead, she made my inner self feel like I too couldn’t breathe without her. I lived all these years without her. Why was it hard just after finding out about her? I wanted to punch my own heart and see if it could give me some answers. Why was I pulled toward her?

I screamed and told her, “Listen queen of the castle frightening everyone who enters this home, I will not be tortured by you. I am not afraid of you, but believe in my words, I am the fear you have been dreading. I will wake you up and I will make you answer all my unanswered questions. I will prove to you I am the owner of this castle which is my home. Dead or alive, you don’t own it anymore. If you say I have wronged in my previous life, I will prove to you, you are dead and wrong. Hey, you dead woman, why do I feel like I’ve somehow been imprisoned here too, not just you?”

There was a storm brewing inside of my home. The huge parlor had smoke floating inside and a pungent smell was in the air. From nowhere, there was red blood spread all over the floors. Fear griped the whole house. I saw Dirk and Geeta were holding on to one another as they closed their eyes. Out of the blue, a warm feeling took over my soul thinking what a wonderful couple they would make. They argued, they smiled, and they held on to one another when they were scared. I said nothing out loud. Yet I treasured the warm feeling of good and love, and I let the warm feeling enter my soul even if it was short-lived.

I heard the frightened shrieks from within the castle seep all the way outside to the village. The brave and the last few staff members of the castle were fleeing for their life by foot. I stepped on a pool of blood, and the blood became a mirror. On the mirror appeared a black and white wedding photograph. Under my feet, I was looking back at myself, yet I had Linus's face and Maharani was the bride. How I knew that was me was beyond my comprehension.

Somehow, I just knew that was my body, my soul, and my mind but I had Linus's face. I walked backward as I saw my bloody footprints on the wedding picture of the beloved couple. How was it even possible or did I just assume it was my body? No, I was absolutely positive it was my body but why was it Linus's face? I always knew if the fingerprints match, then you are the criminal if found guilty through the matched fingerprints, yet here it was my footprints on the bloody mirror.

THE BLOODY MIRROR

The reverse image,
Looking
Back at me,
Wonders if I am
The culprit
With
A feelingless
And heartless soul.
Or is the reflection
A mirror image of
A person
With a criminal mind,
Body,
And soul,
Not my mind,
Body,
And soul,
As I feel,
I love,
And I know
Wrong and right.
The mirror image
Does not

As it is not
A reflective mirror
But
THE BLOODY MIRROR.

Chapter Five:

Identity Is Lost

"Through the
ocean of life,
we not only
lose our
Earthly
vehicles, but
also our
identity is lost."

awn came knocking on my world as my eyes dripped tears of injustice. I saw the phoenix fly into my home through the open windows. The majestic bird didn't frighten me because I saw my best friend and his wife's face on the bird. The demon had copied the same face and smiled back at me. I didn't know what to assume but thought if Maharani was dead, then the goon must be dead too.

I wondered whether my Linus was related to both of them. It is said in reincarnation, you are born with or around the same people you were with during your last life. Was that the reason he could enter the castle without any trouble? I knew somehow, I was related to Linus, but why was my face different from my last life's face? I knew that was my face somehow. I only prayed that I not be the evil villain from last life or in any lifetime as I could never forgive myself for that. A good soul remains good, and a bad soul gets chances to change, so I assumed the demon didn't even get a chance to be reborn because he was evil. But then why was Maharani also imprisoned in that time period?

I so wished Linus was here so I could ask him to forgive me for anything I had done in any of my previous lives. Inside of my soul, I kept asking myself, never ever would I do any wrong unto anyone. I would remove myself and all my needs and feelings to do right. I would wipe away the blood and never cause anyone to bleed. God forgive me if I had done anything wrong. Please let this life be my redemption and repentance for all the wrong of the last life. I will ask for forgiveness and do my best to remove myself from being the third person in a love story. A love story is between two, not three.

I said out loud, "Forgive me for the sins or mistakes I might have committed in my last life. I would never be the third person in a love story, for if I was, then someone help rip out my page from the diary lost in time."

The phoenix spread its wings, and I saw two phoenixes came out of one. One flew outside, and one remained inside. The bird flew near me as I kept my eyes down and my tears fell uncontrollably onto the blood-covered floor. The wings came and caught my tears. As the bird caught my tears, I saw they became white lilies, white carnations, white daisies, and white roses. The flowers filled up over the red blood, and I was standing on a carpet of white flowers.

Geeta came and sat on the carpet of flowers as she said, "Linus just told us you are innocent. These flowers represent innocence, loyalty, purity, love, fertility, good luck, humility, and strength among other symbolic meanings. All say you are innocent and have been framed. Even if you were the third person, you did nothing wrong. Someone else did."

Geeta walked around each flower and took pictures for more research. I was staring at the flowers and wondered why there was a pool of blood that became a mirror. How was it possible I had Linus's face last life? Then, whose face was I born with this life?

Geeta observed the flowers and said, "The phoenix is here to be with and for you, not against you. Your friend didn't leave. Even after death, he is here. You are somehow related to this love story. I don't know but I also believe Linus is somehow related to this love story through blood. That's why he was able to change the blood to flowers. I believe you two are related innocently. Yes, you are innocent as the flowers are the proof of your innocence."

I listened to a very strong-minded woman who was a medical doctor but also a devout Hindu and a seer. She knew a lot of facts about reincarnation, the afterlife, karma, and even dream interpretation. I was blessed to have her in my team of people who refused to leave because she wasn't afraid of the dark side. She was brave enough to deal with it to the end. The love story was still left to be completed. The chapters were still left to be filled. I only saw blank pages in front of me. On every page, however, I saw the ocean and the dark sense of death, revenge, unfair, and unjust.

I spoke out loud, “Yes, it seems like a love story where I feel like the misunderstood villain and you my love are the beloved who is wanted by two men. I am in my mind the lover and you are my beloved. If I am the villain, then I will erase myself from this love story. Yet I will wait till the end to find out what happened. Innocent I call myself until I can prove I am the guilty. Then, I shall give you back your home and remove myself from this love story.”

Geeta walked past me, shaking her head in disagreement. She was listening to my words as her hands flew up and down trying to either say something or just let me know through sign language that she doesn’t believe I was the evil person.

Suddenly, the phoenix cried loudly as it swept next to me. I saw a sword came flying toward me. The phoenix became Linus as he scooped up the sword with his mouth. There in front of my eyes stood my friend Linus. He had huge wings and the orange beak of a magical bird. For the first time in my life, I saw a miracle take place in front of my eyes. I had to blink quite a few times to make sure I wasn’t imagining, and all of this was really happening.

Linus, the magical phoenix, said in clear words, “No, you will not hurt whom I protect. You need to know the truth, not be buried under the ocean with false fables instead of the true stories. I will never allow you to do unjust because you think you can, or you just want to. Maybe you should learn to see the truth first.”

The sword missed me as Linus the bird caught it and saved my life. Linus looked me in the eyes with his magical bird eyes, yet it was still him, my best friend. He was human but still had the magical phoenix’s looks splattered all over him. I wanted to give him a hug or shake him back to life, yet I knew in between us was the bridge of death. I bent my head backward and placed my hands in a fist, trying to think what I could have done to still have him standing by me. I tried to hide my emotions within my soul, but my tears kept failing me.

Linus was dressed like a knight, except his knightly attire was all royal blue and orange. It matched his amazing wings that just were on his back.

Linus looked at me directly and said, “God gives life and takes life. God forgives and punishes. Who are the dead or the living to decide another’s fate? Believe in yourself and solve the unsolved puzzle before you judge yourself. Within your hands I only found love and friendship, and I will be with you till the end, proving your innocence. As you solve your previous life's love story, please solve my wife's and my murder mystery too."

My buddy was talking to me so clearly. How could I bring him to me, or maybe go to where he was? I only ask my God, I ask You, why is there a bridge between we the living, and Your creation, the dead? I won't judge Your work my God, but please help us understand this mystery because watching my best friend in the land of the dead is too painful for my soul.

Linus was watching me with a very sad face as he said, "I will be here whenever you need me. I see you even if you don't see me. Feel me in your heart. I am never far away. God gave this gift as I am still here in this form when you need me. I love you my friend, my brother, and only family I ever needed, have, and shall always have. Even death won't separate us. We are forever conjoined through our bond. My love for you and your love for me shall keep us in an eternal bond throughout eternity. Death is nothing compared to our love."

The tears betrayed me as I knew what he was feeling too. He would have never left me if he could have chosen his path. People write novels about two souls, but they forget the love story of brothers and friends that last eternally.

The morning sun was drenching the castle interior as I saw Dirk and Geeta open the windows and doors of the castle. Fresh smell of breakfast muffins, waffles, and eggs swept into the parlor of the castle. It was strange how the food was being made as I thought everyone left. I knew my other best friend would never leave me as he too would want to take vengeance for our Linus's death.

I walked into the kitchen and saw the other half of the phoenix turned into a human just like Linus. I saw she too had the face of a human and a bird somehow. I wanted to go and hug my sister and hold her there within my embrace for a while.

Even though she was not facing me she said in her clear voice, "No, don't touch me because you will get burned. I love you too much to even think I might cause you any physical or emotional harm. I will be here whenever you need me, your food and all the necessities will be met through us. This is a miracle as God has given us a chance to be here and see through the end of the story. Our daughters need to know their parents did not die in vain but fought even after death. Maybe God will be merciful, and we just might be able to touch our living friends and see our daughters."

Alala was wearing a royal blue smocked dress with layers of embroidery. She looked like a princess as her dress glided, floating above the ground she walked on. Her feet had sandals made from seashells. They looked amazing on her. I wondered how Linus and Alala were there as I thought after death, only souls related to a specific family could travel to the family. Oh my God, how were Linus and Alala connected to this story? Were they really related by blood to anyone here?

Alala read my mind as she smiled and said, “This house is where Linus was born in his previous lives. Always murdered too soon, but we knew of this prophecy through our dreams. So, we married and had the twins. This time by God’s grace, we had girls. That demon can’t touch any daughter born in Linus’s lineage as Maharani is also a female. Sons could be killed but not daughters. That was the only prayer Maharani was granted after a thousand years of praying.”

Alala was so efficient with her hands. I saw how quickly she prepared everyone’s food and still spoke so elegantly. Her footsteps could not be heard but I could somehow smell her moves.

Alala said, “Maharani’s sisters were harmed by him. I don’t know anything else other than how Linus was her biological son in her previous life. He is the reincarnation of her biological son. From him in this life, the lost twin flames will reunite. We don't know how, but maybe through your hands. We only know you are the innocent and if this love story had a name other than the dead Maharani's story, it would be the innocent."

I didn't feel innocent. Instead, I felt like I was the guilty. Our home, the haunted castle, smelled like an all-you-can-eat buffet. The doors to all the rooms were opened, the windows undraped, bed sheets were all changed, and the floors were all mopped and cleaned. I heard the sweet singing and humming of Alala's voice float from a room that hadn't been opened in years. Like a magnetic pull I walked toward the room.

Geeta, Dirk, and a few of the remaining staff members were busy having breakfast. Everything was made by Alala, the magical phoenix. She and her twin flame Linus the magical phoenix, in union did everything. They were together eternally even in death. It felt good in a healthy way. I prayed they remain eternally together. No one feared them or their looks as Geeta chatted about how Alala's twins were doing. She showed Alala pictures of the twins.

I took my morning coffee and went out to inspect the castle. I wondered if there was a room where the projectors were all hiding. Someone would jump out and say this was all a joke for a mystery movie. Yet I asked myself what about my dreams. The dreams I had not shared with anyone, not even Linus. Thinking of Linus made me laugh out loud as he was back as a rising phoenix. I didn't know how long they would be here; however, I had them with me, and forever I would hold them in my heart.

I stopped in front of a solid wooden oak door with a lot of planks. It had mortise and iron hinges. It also had a lot of brass and cast-iron fixtures. I heard this door wasn't opened by anyone as the last inhabitant was Maharani, the Dead Queen herself. I didn't know how to touch the door or open it as I feared what laid behind the door. I almost knocked on the door, then decided no it's my house and this should be my room. My life, my way. No one could tell me what to do or not to do.

I spoke to the Dead Queen and told her, "Dear Maharani, I come in peace. I don't have any intention of separating twin flames. You are dead and if he is your twin flame and dead too then maybe somehow, I can unite you two. I just need to know how I'm involved and who I am in this love story. If I'm the third person, then I will donate this home to you and declare this as a haunted castle so no one will ever enter. This would give you privacy for eternity."

I heard no replies. I knew I didn't need permission to enter my own home. I opened the very old and heavy wood door. It had a hand-carved image of a king with a crown on his head that had nine stones. By his side, sat his queen. On her lap, was a baby boy with a crown on his head showing he was the next heir to the throne. I touched the carving and felt a jolt come out from the carving to my hands. I wondered why this carving seemed so familiar.

The room was dark and smelled like death or maybe mold, or gas, and who knows what else. I understood no one wanted to open this room or get in here for obvious reasons. In front of me, by the very dusty and cobweb filled fireplace, stood a woman dressed in a white, long maxi dress with small blue and pink flowers. On her head, gracefully sat a huge crown. The crown had nine small moonstones and resembled the image carved on the door. Maybe the child in the carving was a girl, not a boy, who was next in line for the throne.

I didn't see seven stones, like the seven-color concept popularized by Sir Isaac Newton. He had split the light spectrum into seven different parts to match the seven musical notes and the mystical lucky number seven. Yet here, there were nine moonstones. Maybe nine was Maharani's lucky number. Or maybe because the number nine is associated with new beginnings and universal love.

Each stone on the crown was a bit different. The stones were in different shades. It looked like there were colorless, white, gray, green, brown, peach, black, blue, and rainbow shimmers. I wondered why my mysterious queen had moonstones on her crown. Maybe it was to represent her dark side. Or maybe she was trying to say she wasn't evil. The stones had something in them that was so familiar to me, yet again it was `something I had never seen in this life before.

Maharani said with a very soft singing voice, "You have finally come back my love. How long I have waited for you. Look! I am almost ready to have the babies. You know, I am going to have two boys. I saw in my dreams, I will have twin boys, but my father is against us. I know I will have my boys even if my father says I will not. He will have someone murder my children because I married the prisoner."

Then, everything changed. The day was different. It was almost dark, and a storm was brewing outside. I saw a woman standing by the window wearing all black. She wore a black maxi gown. Her dress had black lace which dragged on the floor. She was wearing the same crown on her head, yet she was frantically shaking in fear. Her sobs were swallowed within her mouth. Tears were running down her cheeks. The burden of her sorrows was so heavy, she couldn't even raise her hands to wipe her tears.

She watched the ocean as tears poured out of her eyes like a waterfall, and she screamed in a room by herself, "You took away my child, Father! Why? My husband you say is dead, but then why are you taking away the last symbol of my love story? I will take revenge for my husband even if it means I must become a prisoner of this castle for a thousand years, like he too was a prisoner."

A woman entered the room. She was elderly and came in with a basket of bread. She went to Maharani and gave her the basket. I saw Maharani take out a child from the basket and breastfeed the child secretly. I turned away to give them privacy.

She kissed the child's head and whispered, "Take him away from here. Please raise him as your own and make sure no one ever knows he is alive. Name him and all his future sons Lysandros. I want my Lysandros to be reborn from this child again. I will come again from a nearby castle to unite with him as I die. Even death does not touch me as I am so unlucky. Why would the Grim Reaper want to take me upon his boat? He cares not for unlucky people like me."

Maharani was frantically crying as she held her newborn child, the son who was not taken by the Grim

Reaper, as he survived. Maharani placed the child near her chest, and she kissed him frantically. She kept him in her arms, and it seemed like if she could, she would have hidden him within her soul, where no one could touch him. Then, she handed the child back to the elderly woman.

She then whimpered and said, "Aunt Valery, promise me, you will keep my words. Even if I am not reborn, I will watch over you and all your future generations for my Lysandros to be reborn repeatedly until I can avenge his death. Please give me your word."

I saw the woman who looked so familiar look around herself as if she was scared as she said, "Let me name the child Linus, not Lysandros. Maybe then we can hide your last symbol of love. For I believe your Lysandros will come from or around him. All you must do is find him, as your Lysandros will look just like himself as all children from Linus will look like him. Look! This child looks just like your Lysandros, yet I will call him Linus."

It was then a lightning bolt struck the window and under its light, I saw my mother was standing in front of me. She had a basket in which she had a child. She walked outside and I knew she was going to be on the next available ship, so she could take the baby far away from this horrific castle. I wondered about the irony, how I had given the children of Linus to her even in this life.

Maharani went to the window, touched the window, and said, "Oh the blessed ocean, please keep my child, who was murdered, safe within your womb. Protect my son. I love him so much that I sent him away to save him and our future lineage. I will take revenge Father for all the unjust you have committed against me, my beloved, my children, my sisters, and all the other innocent victims. How could you allow your own married pregnant child to be raped and ruined by your goons and just stand and watch? You want to touch me, but I will take my own life if you even try to touch me. I promise."

I walked in front of the fireplace where there was a huge black and white portrait of the man Maharani called Father. There in front of me was my worst nightmare. I saw myself staring back at me. A man with a sword in his hands was sitting on a black horse with a black crow on his shoulder. His smile from within the frame froze my whole interior. Suddenly, I felt like I was dropping sharply from a roller coaster downward without any brake. Everything was upside down. A hand grew from inside of my soul, ripping my chest into halves. Oh God, was I the villain of this love story?

I knew and heard of incest, rape, and murder because so many fathers would rape their own daughters, but I never witnessed this forbidden sin in my life. I knew this person could never be me. My mind, my body, or my soul would never permit myself to any of these grave sins. I would spend all my power and my might to help all whom I could around the world to fight and end these grave sins.

I fell to the ground and broke down as I wanted to take my own life. I didn't want to carry the burden of this sin. Linus, Alala, Geeta and Dirk stood in the room next to me. I believe they all walked into the room when I wasn't looking.

Dirk was shaking as he said, "We saw everything like we were watching a historical silent motion picture from the past as there was no sound. We could make out everything though. Oh God, it's as if the past inhabitants are reliving these horrible events every single day. Oh my God, it's so dreadful."

I told them everything I saw and heard. I sat on the ground as everyone looked at the portrait on the wall.

Then, I heard my Linus the phoenix say, "In each reincarnation story, a puzzle is always missing. I am Linus the son. You are Lysandros. That man is the brutal King whose name is Villainous, the breeder of incest, not Lysandros."

Linus walked and with each step, I saw his wings changed colors. They were magical and from within each part, they glowed with different embers of colors. I couldn't take away my eyes from his wings.

Linus smiled as he then said, "Villainous for whatever reason has your face, but he is not you. I promise I will figure this out before my time is over. Remember, he had three daughters. Two supposedly committed suicide. Maharani, the youngest, fought for her right. She became queen after her sisters passed away, and their cause of death still to this day remains a secret. Even though they took their life in the public, they did not commit suicide. You are not him. Your identity is lost in the ocean of rebirth."

I stood up and knew I must fight for the truth and whatever it was, I would tell the story of a woman feared by all because she fell in love. Two sisters committed suicide and the reason was unknown, yet it seemed like everyone knew what happened. Even if I was the only man in the world of death and life, I would tell her tale and bring her justice.

I prayed to God, and I said out loud, "Jesus, Mary, and Joseph, help and guide me. I don't believe I am or ever could be that evil. Please, if I was reborn, my religion doesn't guide me to reincarnation, but if so, then give me the complete truth."

I knelt and continued to pray as I saw everyone in the room was praying in their own ways. Such is the power of a prayer that I felt energetic just from knowing I could still pray for myself, Linus, Alala, and Maharani.

I said out loud, "I never practiced religion, never divided between religions, but I know there is one Creator. Please guide me. My mother never leaves the house without her rosary. She gave me my cross and rosary to always wear. Please protect me from my own evil sins if there were any. Oh God, I saw my mother was also there in my last birth. I wonder who she was. Somehow in the ocean of death and birth, I believe my identity is lost."

IDENTITY IS LOST

The cold river flows
Across lands
As it changes names.
The roads at different
Four-way intersections
Change their names.
The Earth circles the sun
As it changes
From day to night,
I ask You the Creator,
Through reincarnations,
Different births and different lives,
We the humans
With mortal bodies
Change our identities not by choice,
But as we are given at birth.
So, is it not true,
Even in this birth
Without all my memories,
Without all the facts,
All the truth,
I too can say my
IDENTITY IS LOST.

Chapter Six:

Switched Faces Not Souls

"Bodies die
as they switch
clothes, yet
could souls
accidently
wear the
wrong clothes
and have
switched faces
not souls?"

The skies were restless. The moon forgot to smile back at the Earth and guide everyone to dawn. At first, it was partially obscured, and a glowing halo appeared that looked mystical. In between, I could see some scattered glows behind the night clouds. The overcast sky kept all the glowing candles of the night in the dark. The moon was completely invisible as the clouds blocked the reflected sunlight, just like they blocked the sun's light. It wasn't that they weren't there.

I wondered how powerful the darkness was that it even hid the biggest star of the skies until the battle of the night ended and the sun declared victory. The sun would then smile, overjoyed with victory, and greet the world at dawn. His consort moon would smile back at him and say after a long night, victory is theirs. That's the love story of the sun and moon.

I feared the bridge of life and death placed Maharani to sleep and kept me awake, trying to figure out what happened in our last life. I knew my Dead Queen was having a nightmare even after death. I was going through the same nightmare even when I was still awake. Who said one must fall asleep to dream or have nightmares? You, my dear, had fallen asleep eternally and I was still awake, yet we met one another through our dreams, which some might call nightmares.

Oh, my dear queen, was I that bad? Did I harm your honor? Every night, I see myself running after my Dead Queen. No, I never feared you like the world did, but I feared myself as the person in the mirror and the person inside my soul were different. I didn't know who the person was, whose portrait was framed on the walls of this castle.

As we cleaned up the castle, we found in the library there were more portraits of my face. I hated looking at myself in the mirror, so I stopped looking at mirrors. The working crew thought I framed my own picture in black and white and dressed up in olden day royal tunics to look like a mad king. Yes, they said I looked like a very angry and mad king. There were also portraits everywhere of Linus holding Maharani in his embrace. Every time I saw a portrait of Linus with Maharani, I felt jealous but then had a good feeling as I knew somehow my Linus was a descendant of Maharani.

Thousand-year-old portraits, paintings, sculptures, and mosaics exist in various museums. The Venus of Brassempouy, an ivory statuette, and the Venus of Dolní Věstonice, a ceramic statuette, were made over 25,000 years ago. They're amongst the oldest statuettes and were put in the care of museums. What bothered me was how this castle had portraits hanging on walls like a museum.

Nothing in this castle made any sense. It was as if inhabitants from the past were still living in the castle. The present and the past inhabitants were cohabiting. It was like the past inhabitants never moved on. They adjusted their clothing and all interior furnishings to modern standards. I felt nauseous thinking about how this was happening, but I accepted everything as normal. I wouldn't dare mention any of these thoughts to Dirk, Geeta, or anyone else.

The man in the portrait resembling me was Maharani's evil father. I couldn't be him as then there would be a deadly sin connected to this face, I would not forgive myself for. I didn't blame Maharani for trying to ruin me. The other mystery that bothered me was why the crown was on the head of Lysandros who looked like Linus, not on Maharani's head.

I walked downstairs as we were getting furniture from the coach house up to the main house. Geeta made interior decorating her job as well. I saw even through all the horrific events, Geeta was spending a lot of time with Dirk. He wore a pair of old jeans and a blue t-shirt which said Tasmania. Geeta wore a white midi dress which she brought with her to the island. Dirk with his blue eyes and blond hair and Geeta with her long black hair and brown eyes looked like a couple from my romance novels. They were a perfectly matched and amazingly beautiful couple. It felt good to see a love story being written even in the horrifying castle and that love still lives even in the darkest part of the world.

I went for a night stroll wearing my favorite plaid shirt and blue jeans. The whole village was now familiar with my shirt as I had it on when I first saw Maharani's ghost standing on the hilltop. Tonight, there were a lot of people working through the dark night. It didn't get very cold in this part of the world as we only needed a sweater at times. The yard lights were very bright and supplied what the moon refused to do. It seemed like Ms. Moon too was afraid of me or maybe my face.

I told the moon out loud, "Oh dear moon, I don't blame you. I too would be scared of my face, but I assure you I am good and never will be on the other side."

I walked for a long time, and without even realizing, I somehow walked into a maze of roses. How did these roses survive all these years? As the story went, the rose garden was haunted. No one planted any plants for a thousand years. All the flowers, the fruit trees, and the evergreen bushes were all still alive and thriving. Maybe they were being taken care of by someone who probably sold the fruits and vegetables. Maybe the person was doing all of these ghostly effects to scare everyone away. I would investigate everything as soon as I could. At least this thought was better than the one I didn't even dare to think.

In the middle of the night, a crown that was so familiar was circling above my head like a vortex, pulling me into the tunnel. I heard bawls and screams coming from the caretaker's cottage on the castle grounds. I bought this two-hundred-acre compound thinking it would be my family's getaway vacation place. I had planned to rent this castle out as a tourist destination spot. So close to Australia and Asia, people would have flocked to vacation here in peace. Yet the horror stories from the dark have traveled all around the globe marking this castle as one of the most haunted and forbidden places on Earth. On various websites, it probably would say to enter at your own risk and return to a normal life could not be guaranteed.

I tried to listen to the sounds of cries yet heard nothing. Then again, I heard whimpers of a woman. I walked into the caretaker's cottage easily as the doors were left ajar. No locks or hinges were on the doors. The cottage had a lantern burning as a woman cried through the dark night.

As her crown shined, I heard her say, "No, Father, please leave me alone! Why are you doing this? You have all the women on the island! Don't touch your own child."

I saw an elderly man all drenched with blood, walk out as he had a sword in his hands. He was twirling in a circle as if he was drunk. He had multiple bottles of alcohol, and he was shaking in anger. He wasn't alone as there was a man with him who had blood all over his body.

The other man said, "I thought you wanted me to just rape your daughter as it gives you pleasure to see that. But death? Murder? I don't want blood on my hands."

The elderly man laughed and walked like a drunk. The other man who looked like a caretaker had an axe one would use to chop trees with. I wanted to rush in and see what was going on, if I could somehow save the woman who was probably dead if not fighting for her life.

I walked into the cottage which looked out to the ocean. I saw a woman all covered in blood was trying to jump into the cold water.

She prayed and told her God, "Forgive me my God for I can't live with this sin. Father had his goon rape me."

I tried to run to her, but my feet weren't moving. I tried to scream, but words were not coming out of my mouth. I prayed and then was able to let out words, yet I wondered if she even heard me. I hated myself for not being able to scream when I needed to do so.

I then somehow did scream as I told her, "For God's sake, do not jump. Life is very long, and nothing is worth giving up on life. Please believe me and give life a chance."

The young woman looked at me and tilted her head toward my right. I saw behind me walked in Linus.

He was crying and said, "Divya, please don't take your life. Hold my hands. I will take revenge for this and fight against your powerful father. I just need time.. I pray God gives me time to fight and bring justice to this castle and all the unjust that has happened here."

Behind him was Maharani. She was crying and frozen in place. The wind blew her dark hair. Her all-white maxi gown made her look like a night fairy. The moon illuminated her face as I could even see her tears pouring from her eyes. Her eyes were red from crying. Her crown was missing, and her hair was messy on closer inspection. It seemed like she was running in the wind.

Painful cries broke the silence of the quiet night. I heard a distinctive hissing and clashing sound, followed by an excruciating shriek from a woman who was silent within a few seconds. I then witnessed Divya fall backward into the cold deep ocean. She had a sword lunged into her chest that went all the way through her back.

Maharani screamed and said, "Why Father? What did we do to you that you are taking our lives? You get people to rape us, then you have them murder us. Now you will tell the world Divya committed suicide. Why are you doing this? Are you even human? She is your daughter! How could you? Yes, maybe not biological but you raised her. You had a man rape her mother and have her. Then, why did you kill her?"

I knew someone attacked her from a hidden place. The evil father Maharani so feared was not in the room but by the window where the sword came from. I looked outside and saw he was smiling and walking by himself, laughing out loud.

Maharani then turned toward the man who looked like Linus or the demon who pretended to be Linus and said, "Lysandros, please help my sisters. Today, the ocean has taken one of my sisters. Before it takes another one, I want to run away with you in your boat. We can take Vidya with us, so she can be safe."

Maharani sat on the ground that was stained by her sister's blood. She touched it and screamed as she fell to the ground, trying to hug the blood. She was now covered in blood stains as she made a fist and tried to harm herself by punching the window that was left open. The grill on the window was taken out by someone, so that he could kill the girl and make it look like she committed suicide. I saw Maharani was trying to see if she could see her sister. I, however, saw the girl who had been thrown out was now on a boat. She was going home with the Grim Reaper.

Maharani then said, “Lysandros, my mother and my two stepmothers were all killed after childbirth. He forced them to be raped by his workers then he killed them and told everyone, they committed suicide. Now he is saying this castle is haunted and that’s why everyone who enters, goes crazy and commits suicide. Like them, he had my sister killed.”

Lysandros with Linus’s face was shaking as he looked at me directly. I wondered if he saw me or if he was even able to see me. He came close to me and tried to touch me. His hands went toward me but somehow, everywhere he touched felt like a buzzing jolt, causing an involuntary muscle spasm. It was like I was running through a tunnel. I wondered what tunnel it was that I ran through as he touched me. His hands became invisible or mine became like light.

Maharani watched him and said, “Lysandros, why do your hands become invisible when you try to go near the window? Please tell me you are not a warlock or a ghost. Now you are scaring me. I do not ever wish for anyone to become a ghost and live in this horrendous castle with Father the self-proclaimed King Villainous. Did you know the crown does not fit him? It slides off and makes him bleed. He cannot ever wear it."

I saw in the window appeared a lot of small black birds. They were all flying together as birds fly in groups to return home at sunset. Yet it was so late in the night. Why were they crowding the window? I had no clue.

Suddenly Maharani started to cry and said, "I do not care what you are as I have given my love and heart only to you. Please find my sister and bring her back. We need to rush and see where she is. Please! I will not lose my sisters to this kind of unjust. The whole world will think she committed suicide after she had an affair with the gardener. Father will publicly have the gardener executed with charges of rape. Vidya, please don't die! Come back to me! Oh my God! Lysandros, please help me protect Vidya. I believe they will go after her now."

I wanted to tell her what I had seen in the window, but I realized she couldn't even see me. In the dark night, Maharani ran outside trying to walk by the ocean water. Her bare feet were bleeding. She had blood all over her hands as she stood on the hillside of the castle and extended her hands toward the ocean. Her white gown covered in mud and dirt looked completely black as she cried with her bloody hands raised to the ocean. I remembered her doing this before, as the whole island saw her like this. She screamed and cried calling her sister's name. No one responded. Nobody floated up as I believed the force of the ocean water could have taken her sister anywhere.

The blood dripping from her hands mixed with the ocean water. As she just lost her sister, she let all her tears fall into the ocean, shrieking and crying. Oh my God, that's what the islanders saw every night and thought she was haunting everyone. No one realized she was the victim. Her pain was too much for me to bear as I watched her stare at her husband's face. They just spoke with their eyes.

The man she called her husband frantically was searching under the cold freezing ocean water and the rocks with a lantern. He then waved the lantern toward the water as we all saw a boat appear from nowhere. The boat I had seen before was there for everyone to see. I knew the Grim Reaper was waiting in the water for a while. Maybe he just sat there always and only was visible when he took a person on his boat.

Maharani's husband stood in the water as the boat came near him. Inside of the boat we saw clearly in the moon's glow was the Grim Reaper. He had his scythe, a large, curved, harvesting type tool, in his hands. He wore a long flowing black robe with a hood. I saw his face as he looked at me directly. I got off balance as I walked backward seeing the skeletal face of the Grim Reaper. Somehow, he knew I was visiting a place normally people never enter.

Maharani walked toward him and said with tears pouring like a fountain from her eyes, "Why are you doing this unjust to me? Don't you have a heart? She did nothing wrong, but the world will fear her and this castle to be haunted. Why? I promise to you when my time comes for me to be on your boat, I will haunt this castle eternally until justice is found. I challenge you to a battle then and only then. Even if I die, I will not come to your boat as I will take revenge for all the unjust that has been done here by one man's sin and greed."

The Grim Reaper just stared at her and said nothing. He raised his head toward the skies as we saw a tunnel of light appeared. The boat and all its inhabitants including Divya disappeared within the churning tunnel that also resembled a staircase which connected the ocean to the skies. For the first time in my life, I was witnessing a supernatural phenomenon. Maharani jumped into the cold water as I watched her husband rush in and take her out. She lay on the ground and fainted from all the horrific events of the cold dark night.

Her husband was trying to get her to wake up as he held her in his arms and cried with her in his arms. He sat holding on to her patiently as he took off his shirt and placed it on her. I saw there were chain marks on his body like he was in prison chained up. It's so strange that I have those chain marks on my body too, at the same exact places.

My mother had said to me, "Oh Lysandros, you were born with these chain marks. These were your birth marks. I believe you were chained and imprisoned in your last birth. So even in this life, you have the same marks."

Lysandros, the husband of Maharani, walked with her in his arms to an underground door of the castle. The moon's shimmering light showed me a man from a thousand years ago carrying the same marks I've carried on my body since birth. He knew how I got them even though I still didn't know.

Maharani jumped up and saw her husband staring at her as she said, "Lysandros, who are you? Why did your hands disappear and reappear in the window just before this incident. Are you a demon or maybe a ghost? I know the hunters who work for my father saw your hands disappear. Rumors will spread I am married to a demon. Then, they will say you did all of this. I had a dream years ago that I was married to a human, and I was a ghost. Everyone called me the Dead Queen. Maybe dreams are reverse, and you are the ghost, the dead king, and I am the mortal."

The night could not have gotten any worse as then we heard screams of a woman come from the castle tower. We were in the lowest part of the castle, and the screams came from the highest part of the castle. To run upstairs would take forever as I watched Maharani frantically trying to see what was going on.

The lantern in the lighthouse was glowing, but the light became dim. I knew someone had dimmed the lantern as I heard screams of a woman coming from the tower and spreading across the whole island. Yet no one said anything. No one came forward to investigate against their demon king. Everything became quiet. There were no crying sounds, no whimpering sounds, no fear, and no pain. I saw a man was standing in the lantern room as he was looking out toward the ocean. The man was my mirror image. I felt like I was looking into a mirror through the ghostly glow of the moon on his face.

I watched Maharani run toward the castle as did her husband. It was then a body fell from the tower room into the deep ocean. The body made no complaints as the soul from the body had already left all the pain and fear behind as only memories. No sounds were uttered from the dead body of Vidya. We all knew she was gone while the ruthless father watched his daughter be raped and killed, the exact same way he had killed all other women. I wondered what was in him that allowed such demonic behaviors. He stood and watched his daughters get brutally raped and be killed, but he never touched them.

Maharani walked to the ocean side as she waited for the Grim Reaper to arrive with his boat. I didn't know how I knew her mind. I felt like I could read her thoughts. She stood up and said nothing as again the Grim Reaper appeared and took Vidya. I watched Maharani shiver in anger and with revenge piling up from sorrow-filled anguish. She again spread her hands covered from the blood she picked up as she touched and kissed the ground that was covered with blood from her sister. Her husband was standing there trying to comfort his wife.

He said, "I will take revenge for this castle and all the innocent inhabitants of this castle until justice is served. I will not rest, my love, until I find justice for your sisters, your mother, and your stepmothers. All the women who were brought here and were subjected to rape, sexual assault, and could not live to even defend or tell their stories will find justice through my story if not in one life, then in another life. I will be reborn over and over again to take revenge."

Maharani laughed and cried at the same time as she watched her husband for a while. Rain started to pour down and she was getting drenched. Her hands were still covered in blood as even the pouring rain couldn't wash away the blood from her hands.

She looked above the skies and said, "My sisters do not know how to swim. They were not my stepsisters, but the only family I had on Earth. Please God, tell me why you are taking away all the family members I have. If it is my sin, then let me suffer, but not them as they did nothing wrong. I married and I went against Father. They did not."

It was then a lightning bolt hit the ground all around us. Maharani's husband looked directly at me. He tried to blink and clear his eyes. I tried to look directly at him, yet I wasn't able to see his face. Every time I tried to see his face, I saw a mirror on his face and my own reflection looking back at me. Was this real? Was this really happening? What was going on? I thought it to be strange as I knew he looked like Linus, but I could only see the mirror and in the mirror,

I saw my reflection. I saw the face of Maharani's father looking back at me.

Maharani's husband said, "Oh dear, I see a man in front of me, a ghost. I see in front of his face there is a mirror and I see myself in the mirror."

Her husband walked forward and tried to touch me. As another lightning bolt appeared, our hands touched. There seemed to be one pair of hands as I saw my hands existed and his hands were missing. I knew he was in the past and I was in the present, but then why did I have Maharani's father's face. I knew I had to be patient and let the story take its course.

Maharani walked toward her husband and pulled him toward her. In front of them, a lot of people appeared. They all had lanterns and axes in their hands. Everyone was looking at her husband.

Maharani screamed, "He killed my sisters! My father killed my sisters! He is a murderer and had them raped and murdered. He lies and spreads rumors saying they committed suicide. I witnessed all of it firsthand. He is a demon. Please believe me! He is a demonic king who must be stopped at any cost!"

All the people watched her, and they screamed in union, "She is a witch and the man she is with is a demon.

His body was missing just a while ago. His hands disappeared and then reappeared. Stop her! She is a demonic woman who is wearing all black and has blood on her hands! She also has the king's crown on her head!"

Maharani screamed and tried to explain, but no one was listening. They were all throwing stones at her. People were throwing crosses at her too. It was like Maharani was being set up to look like an evil queen. Her husband jolted in front of her and wrapped his arms around her petite body, protecting her from everything that was being thrust at her. The stones and crosses hit her husband who was bleeding. The strangest part was wherever he was hit, blood was gushing out of my body. I didn't feel bad. The pain didn't bother me as my soul was glad to be able to protect her even for a while.

Maharani then said, "I am not wearing his crown. This crown came from beneath the ocean. It keeps coming to me because it belongs to my husband. It is his family crown. It has his family's seal of the nine moonstones on it."

She held the crown in her hands as she tried to show them. I saw her husband tried to stop her as he whispered something in her ears, but I could not hear. She shook her head and said no to him. Only he could hear as did I.

Someone shouted like a crazy man, “It is some kind of sorcery. He is a sorcerer. He came on a ship from somewhere and is trying to do evil acts. He has placed Crown Princess Aarna under his spells. She will be imprisoned by him eternally and this castle will be under a horrific spell. I am telling all of you to beware. She will die just like her sisters. They all committed suicide. Maybe the gardener didn’t rape them, but he probably did. Let’s get him killed and her with him, so our peaceful King Villainous can rule in peace. His demonic daughters and wives have ruined his reputation and honor.”

The man who was leading the crowd to go against Maharani was the same man who raped her sisters. An innocent woman was being framed to be feared and known as the evil Dead Queen. I knew I was the problem as I somehow traveled time and caused this horrific mess. Yet I knew I must save the woman from the man who looked like me by hook or crook. So, I took a step back and hid behind the trees. I told myself not to show myself to them at any cost.

Maharani screamed and shouted at everyone, “He is my husband, so he is your king! My father rules no more because I am of age. The law was he would rule until I am of age and so I am. You all will listen to me, Maharani

Aarna. I tell you he is a human. He is neither a demon nor a sorcerer. This storm is fooling all your eyes. My sisters were killed and thrown into the ocean by my father. I want my father to be arrested. He is the demon who has been terrorizing everyone."

The scenery changed. I was thrown from one scene to another. This was getting really nauseating. I watched a very scared Maharani run through a forest. She was saying something. I couldn't hear her words, but knew she was out of breath. She had a breadbasket in her hands as she was talking with a woman.

I heard the woman say, "Never fear my Queen, your son will be safe with me. I will take him far away in this ship. My friend will take me with him, and we will raise this boy as our own son. I feel sorry for your twin son who was murdered by your father. It is good your father did not know you had twins. As promised, I will name your and Lysandros's son Linus."

I wondered if her husband had my name and their son's name was Linus. What was her father's name? Villainous? Or was that a nickname given to him as obviously he was the villain of his time. I couldn't find any record of him or his name online or in history books. I wondered why. Everything before Maharani was wiped off from the pages of history. All that remained was an evil ghost queen known to all as the Dead Queen.

I walked into another room in the dark foggy night. This night seemed to never end and was taking me through a horrific maze. I saw a very elderly man in torn clothing was trying to touch Maharani. I ran toward her and screamed at the elderly man to stop and leave her alone.

I screamed, “King Lysandros, the husband of Maharani, please come and help her! She needs you tonight!”

In front of me, I saw clearly under the moon’s glow, a man standing who looked like Linus. He was shackled in chains. His feet were covered with heavy river rocks, and his body was bleeding from torture. Maharani was wearing her long black gown with a slit. From behind, I saw her mesmerizing dark hair was glittering like the stars. When I saw her face, however, I saw a woman in pain with red swollen eyes and quivering lips that were bleeding from biting. I learned my lesson to never judge a person from the back.

She lifted her head up and said, “Dear beloved husband, please know I never betrayed our love. Our child was murdered by my father as he has sent this goon to rape me. My father escaped from prison and is in that closet hiding. He watched that man attempt to rape me, but God as my witness, I fought with my life. I will take my life and be a prisoner of this castle eternally until you free me, but I will not allow that man to touch me. I did not allow him to touch me, I promise."

I screamed as did the man in shackles as he moved very slowly with a lot of weight on his body. He held the elderly man with his shackles. I held his hands, so it was easy for him to maneuver his hands. I tried to stay close to Maharani's husband as I saw she had so many questions in her eyes.

I wondered what had happened from last time they were together to now. When did she get pregnant and give birth? I realized I was seeing glimpses of their past. I only wanted to see if I could somehow save them both. I tried to do something but felt helpless. Yet again, time had passed, and I appeared at another event which was in action in front of me. I didn't know what happened in the past, but I had to make do with the little glimpses I was able to witness.

Maharani's father came out shouting and screaming. His face was red. His veins were visibly popping. The man was shaking in anger. I knew whatever his defense was, he was all evil. Not a single bone in his body was good.

He yelled, "I have never raped any one of my daughters, but I enjoyed watching you all get ruined. Now let me murder your husband so I can keep you a prisoner of mine eternally in this castle. I love watching you all get what you asked for. I actually did all of you a favor. Just like my mother, you all are whores who have asked for it."

There in front of my eyes, spears were flying in all directions. The thud and the crunch from the spears striking the wooden shields could be heard as blood was pouring from dead bodies all around. I could barely keep up with the ongoing occurrences I was witnessing. My heart rate was increasing. I worried why my watch still hadn't given a high heart rate alert.

I witnessed Maharani's father take out a sword that looked royal. The sword had a symbol of a crown. He thrust the sword through Maharani's husband's chest. He had a smirk on his face and was proud of what he was doing. Maharani's husband fell backward into the dark deep ocean. He closed his eyes and asked me to help him. I gave him my hand as he was frozen in the air watching Maharani's father.

I held on to him with all my force, but a sound distracted me. I saw the evil man take out a child from a closet. The same woman I saw earlier who escaped with the child came out in shackles. The child was a newborn baby wrapped in a blanket which had a crown symbol on it. On the right cheek, the child had a birthmark. It struck me that my buddy Linus had the same birthmark. I had to jolt myself back to why I was there. I needed to stay focused and not drown in my own thoughts. I realized my reason for being there was not to save Maharani or her husband who looked like Linus, but the baby.

The woman said, “He caught me and murdered my husband in the ocean. He took the baby and has been punishing me ever since. I promise I will kill you! You evil demonic king! How could you murder a child? The child of Lysandros and Maharani will live. That is my dying wish.”

Maharani’s husband tried to touch his son as he and I separated our hands.

He said to me, “Please save our son. He is also your son as you and I are the same person in different time periods. It matters not if I die, but please let my son live.”

I took the baby and held him with all my might. In front of me, I witnessed a miracle. An invisible see-through man from the future was saving his bloodline from the past. My reasoning for time traveling was now clear.

I watched Lysandros from the past pull Maharani’s father with him as he fell into the deep ocean.

He said, “With our death, Maharani will live as I will save her even in my death.”

The evil king laughed like he was having fun. He signaled for Maharani’s husband to watch in the direction he was pointing. Just before both fell, Maharani’s father pierced Maharani in the chest with his sword. She fell backward onto the cold grounds of the castle floor.

She cried and said, “My beloved, please take me with you to the bottom of the ocean. I want to be buried with you. If I am reborn, then I want to come back and be only yours. Oh my God, please let this evil demon father of mine be punished eternally in Hell. I will punish him even in a ghost form if I must.”

I was drowning in the deep blue ocean and couldn’t breathe. I knew this was not a dream as I had seen this part in my dreams so many times. I was drowning and saw next to me was Maharani’s father. I wondered how I thought I was drowning when in the moon’s reflection I saw it was Maharani’s husband, the man with Linus’s face. Yet for the first time, I knew it was my soul and he was my past. I could feel my life was leaving my body.

I saw Maharani’s father was staring at me under the water. He was smirking and smiling like he knew something I didn’t. I watched him and saw his life was being sucked out from his body, as was mine. I thought of Maharani and knew she was waiting for me or rather the man dying who was me yet had the face of Linus. I saw my soul rise as did Maharani's father's soul, and I realized he was doing something evil.

As I walked toward the reincarnation tunnel, he said, "Switch faces now with me you fool. That is how you will be reborn with my face, and I will have yours. I am the most powerful demon that died, and I will live eternally. You, stupid fool, will be reborn with my face and shall be hated by Maharani forever. I hate your life for you because you are the most pathetic soul."

As I walked into the tunnel, he dived back into the ocean. Then, I saw in his hands, he carried a mirror where I saw my face and his face were intertwined. I watched Maharani's father's face become my face as my face became his.

I cried and told my God, "Why is it You have given so much power to demonic figures? How is it fair that I will be reborn with his face, and she will forever hate me?"

Everything was becoming fuzzy. I knew I didn't have much time, yet I wanted to hold on for as long as I could. If it was going to be my last feeling, then I wanted to hold on to something positive.

I heard my past body say, “I am blessed to know my future generations will continue through our baby boy Linus. Thank you, my God, for this gift. I will accept in exchange whatever punishments I must go through. I pray my beloved Maharani sees me through her soul, not through the face in the mirror.”

I was so happy as I realized my buddy Linus was not just the direct lineage of my son Linus, but my baby boy’s reincarnation. His daughters were of our lineage. I felt my life was being sucked out through a whirlwind tunnel. The feeling was so painful. I never thought my soul from this life could sense the painful death from my last life.

I did, however, sense the painful death. I felt like I just went through the tunnel of death accompanied by all the pain, suffering, and fear of not being able to see or hear my beloved wife and tell her I would never stop loving her, even after death. Remember me, my beloved, even if you don’t recognize me, let our love be your guide as the demon has switched faces not souls.

SWITCHED FACES NOT SOULS

Oh,
My precious,
My beloved,
My sweetheart,
I take this vow.
Tonight,
I will
Teach you love.
I will
Show you
How to recognize
Through the inner soul,
Not with
Your deceiving eyes,
As you love from
Your inner soul,
Your blind faith,
And your twin flame's
Inner fires.
Let this lover,
Let this beloved,
Let this twin flame
Display,

Exhibit,
And present
To you,
Love not
With your eyes,
But your inner sight,
As this twin flame has
SWITCHED FACES NOT SOULS.

Chapter Seven:

Who Am I

"Oh my
beloved,
through your eyes,
I know who
I was,
yet within
your eyes,
I wonder if
you know
who am I?"

The bitter taste of death filled with regret and what ifs crowded my soul. Death did not frighten me, but being separated from my beloved was worse than death. Just one more time, I wanted to hold her, my beloved wife, and tell her, "No matter what the world says and thinks, I love you. Maybe our love story won't find any place in the pages of history or be bound into a book. Within my soul, however, our love story will be kept safely for eternity. Oh my God, I only wished I could have had both my sons with me. Forgive me my sons, Linus and my twin boy who forever shall remain nameless."

The cold freezing ocean water ripped the soul out of my body. The cold shocked me. I was instantly gasping for air. Then, a sensation of burning jolted through my entire body like someone was giving me some kind of electric shock. There were painful pinches that poked me in every direction through my body. I was shivering and just wanted to sleep and forget all the troubles of life.

My entire body went numb, and I tried to shake myself and wake my body up. Yet all I felt was numbness and weakness. I heard my mother was upset and crying for me. She was calling me and wrapped a warm blanket around my body. I knew I was being called to wake up and come back to my own body in my own time by someone who must love me like my mother does and wasn't ready to let go of me.

I opened my eyes. Geeta was looking down at my face from very close by. She was all bent over as I lay on top of the cold wet grass. It was a very uncomfortable situation. I saw a very panicked Geeta screaming at my face. Everything was becoming clear, but I felt the ocean water and just wanted to fall asleep.

Someone was asking someone else for help. I wondered who was calling me. Was it Geeta? It sounded like a man's voice. I tried to open my eyes again and I heard Dirk frantically screaming. In a split second, I realized if anybody was capable of waking the dead, it was him.

My buddy Dirk was crying and shouting as he whimpered, "Oh no! You don't get to die on me! I already lost one buddy who flies around as a phoenix now. Don't you go on dying! What do you want to be after your death? A king with wings? Now get up and act normal. We can plan when we will die and how. Maybe the seer could tell us when we will die. That way, there will be no surprises. Get up Lysandros and shake it off!"

I tried to get up. I saw the memories of how I looked identical to Maharani's evil demonic father. Somehow, I knew he was happy knowing he succeeded in separating us in death and rebirth. The face my beloved hated was now my face. I was scared to see my own face in the mirror, and I wondered how the others would feel knowing I had the face of a demon. I've heard people say that phrase so easily but maybe it shouldn't be taken lightly. In some weird way, I felt good because I knew the truth. The only fact that could set me free from my own guilt was the truth.

It was then I jumped up and screamed at the top of my lungs, "I am not evil! Neither am I a demon, but I have the face of a demon. Through an evil spell, as we were both dying, a demon switched our faces. He couldn't switch our souls, so I came back with his face, and he came back with mine. Or he kept my face wherever he is. I've got my innocent soul, and he still has his demonic soul. I believe he still has his physical body as I still have mine, but he is a shapeshifter."

I felt good to be alive. It was like I had a second chance in life. No one would understand as I was lying on the grass for a while not dead. Yet I felt the pain and horror of death. The feeling ripped open my entire being.

I watched my newly found group of family friends and said, "It seemed as though he didn't want to have my face, but he wanted me to have his face. More likely, he wanted to have my body. He was upset he couldn't have my physical body. There is something about his body that is missing from my memory or maybe I just don't know, but he was very upset. Even after switching faces, he is still missing something. So, he is very upset. I need to figure out what he is hiding about his body."

I jumped up as my inner soul wanted to hold on to my beloved wife. I didn't fear her, nor did I care if she knew who I was or was not. It didn't bother me that our vows had tied us to only one life as I had taken my wedding vows for eternity. I felt tears fall from my eyes as I knew none of this was fair. Why did I go through the reincarnation tunnel if she was left buried in the castle?

I made a fist and wanted to jump into the ocean of death to be with her. Yet I knew my God had His own way and His own time. Who was I to complain? It just tore my whole being apart, but I had to keep my control as everything in life finds its answers through time, sometimes through a thousand years of waiting.

Geeta took my hand as did Dirk. They helped me go inside the castle. All I knew was I changed and had fresh clothes on. Alala brought some hot freshly brewed tea in as I lay in the brand-new king-sized bed in the guest quarters of the castle. The windows were open as were the huge wooden paneled doors that led to the veranda overlooking the ocean. I could hear the waves and its war with the wind from my bed.

The cold freezing water was still pinching my body. I said nothing as I kept the inner pains of my soul secretly hidden within myself. I prayed for my tears to obey my command and not betray my words. Dear tears, please don't let me lose this war.

Geeta walked next to my bed and helped herself up on my bed. She sat very comfortably. Dirk got on the same bed and sat next to her. They were both shaking like they too were going through the same situation I had gone through. How selfish could I be that I became so self-absorbed. I forgot to see what the two were going through. It was fearful for them both as they were witnessing things no living human had ever encountered, at least to my knowledge. I didn't even know if they saw anything, or if I must retell them everything and how much would they believe.

Dirk broke the silence as he said, "Lysandros, that was a ride we all went through. With you, we all traveled to the past. Maybe there is an energy vortex here for which the castle becomes a time portal. Even though we are in the present, we were able to see what happened in the past. I don't know if you realized, but as you walked into each room or even the forest, it was like a live-action movie was playing in front of us. We were all silently witnessing and walking through your dreams. We felt the pain, the jolt, and even being breathless and gasping for air. We were outside of the TV frame whereas you were inside the TV screen."

Geeta shivered again. She stayed silent and allowed Dirk to talk. She was shaking and playing with her fingers. I realized she played with her fingers whenever she was scared or nervous. Dirk held her hands without saying anything. He just looked at her as she too just watched him, and their eyes were locked on one another for a while until she became calmer. I said nothing but again my soul felt so good to witness a love story blossom in front of my eyes.

Dirk continued, "The magical part was we realized we could see everything, but no one could see us. Yes, up to the moment when you drowned and changed faces with the demon. We were on top of the water watching you drown, and the demon had a strange rope he placed around your neck as he uttered some words, and you changed faces with him."

I tried to understand how all of this was even possible. What happened to my child Linus? Was he safe? I still had the guilt of not being able to save his twin brother.

I touched my hair as it still felt wet. My whole body had physical signs of being under water for such a long time.

Dirk then said, "We watched you float away as a newborn baby. The demon walked out with your face and stood by the shore, laughing like a maniac. He didn't enter the tunnel of rebirth, judgment, or Heaven and Hell. I wondered if he as a Catholic entered purgatory but no, he just walked out of the ocean. He was so happy that he was jumping up and down. Suddenly, he looked and touched a certain part of his body. He fell to the ground and was squirming as he screamed 'No!'"

Everyone stopped talking as I saw Alala and Linus standing near the open windows. It was so strange to see Linus through the lens of my newly gathered knowledge. He was my lineage, my son from another birth, and my best friend, my twin from this life. His daughters would be raised by my mother and Aunt Grace. They were the last symbol of Maharani's and my love. Our love story would continue through them. We all knew this truth except for Maharani. She fought to keep her son alive, but she didn't know her suffering and prayers were answered as he survived and had a lineage through those little wonders.

Linus looked at me and for a while I thought he was going to cry or just say let's go home. Whenever he was under pressure or upset, he would go back to Aunt Grace, and he would pull and drag me with him. Linus and I had an inside joke. Someone would try to murder me for my money, so Linus would pretend to be me, and I would pretend to be him. That way, I would be able to pay for his ransom and take him back home with me.

Linus laughed as he said, “Lysandros, as we all witnessed the events with you, I had taken your son Linus and given him to my mother’s ancestors. Maybe you traveled for that one miracle. Even in death, I feel good knowing our daughters lived. We are back here with you, stronger than before. So, God is merciful.”

He then held Alala as I could see they were very happy knowing they did their part in life to make this world a better place. I promised I would do my part and make sure the demon never gets to rule this castle or island ever again.

Linus laughed and said, “Oh buddy, I wish we could pay ransom to someone and be free from all the horrific tales. One more time, just once, I would want to be reborn with my Alala to have a long and healthy life together. I would want to again be your best friend. Yes, I am the reincarnated son of you and Maharani. Now I’m your best friend, back from the ocean of death with the mercy and blessings of God.

Let's make sure this demon doesn't rule Earth or beyond ever again."

I felt a burn inside my soul. It was the inner burning of revenge and the question why. I asked myself how much a person could hate another that they would be waiting to take revenge for a thousand years. The rough ocean touching our island had to remind all of us she was still listening to all our conversations. The furious and irritated ocean didn't feel meditative, calm, or relaxing, but seemed horrific, sad, and angry.

Maybe it's our own feelings we place on the nature around us. I knew a lot of secrets remained buried under the cold and rough ocean bed. I did the Anjali Mudra by placing my hands together. I prayed as I vowed to get to the bottom of this story, even if it meant I must remove one stone at a time from beneath the ocean.

Linus said, "All the details can wait until they come out on their own. Right now, I want to take revenge for what the demon did last life and in this life. He pretended to be me. Since you have his face and I was reborn with your face through our bloodline, he must be a demonic shapeshifter. Demonic figures can take on faces of anyone they wish. So, we must solve this mystery as we unravel the complete story."

Alala was watching the ocean as her wings flapped ever so slightly. She watched her husband and held him with her hands which were beneath her wings. They both were so beautiful. They were magical and their ambiance radiated a magical aura around them. Alala looked at me and laughed as I knew somehow, they could both read minds.

She said with her sweet musical voice, "No, I can't read minds, but I can hear some words when people are thinking. I wanted to say, I wonder why the demonic character never raped me or even tried to. I am blessed he did not, yet I only wonder if he even can or maybe something is missing and that's why he gets other men to rape women for him. He gets satisfaction from watching them. This is weird but I somehow feel like he just might be missing his male part."

Geeta was again playing with her hands. She was Googling something on her phone. I knew she was trying to see if there was any information about this evil man on the web. I pondered if there was some truth to Alala's thought as Maharani and her sisters were from three different mothers, yet they didn't look anything like their father at all.

Oh my God, what if he married women but because of some kind of physical reason, he couldn't consummate the marriages? So, he hired men to rape his wives. Then, he killed each one so there would be no one to testify or say anything against him. I just didn't know how a man could go through this horrendous act. I said nothing out loud because I kept having a weird feeling as to how the demonic king succeeded in giving me his face. He disappeared into the underworld with my face and a shapeshifting body.

As we were all talking, Dirk gestured to all of us to be quiet. Alala and Linus went invisible right in front of us. We watched then during the very sunlit dawn, Maharani walked toward the guest bedroom I was staying in. She stood in the middle of the hallway as she tried to enter but stopped her feet because she knew something was wrong.

I knew the room was original. There were a lot of renovations being done in the castle. I wondered if she could tell or see all the renovations. Or was she stuck in her time period? I could ask but decided not to as I didn't want her to have a panic attack. Maharani was using a cane unlike herself.

She walked in and said, "Husband, are you here? I have been waiting for you for so long. Even time betrays me, like everyone else. I wake up or go to sleep and still everything is the same. Please keep your promises and touch my eyes, so I can see you all over again. Maybe you died and are traveling as a spirit. I will take revenge for your death. How could I still be alive if my twin flame is dead?"

Maharani walked near the window, and I realized she couldn't see. She was blind, yet somehow, she knew where things were and followed her basic instincts. I followed her footsteps and knew I had to delay this union even though my heart so wanted her to know I was her Lysandros. I walked far away from her and thought she wouldn't realize.

I remembered I was not the ghost, but she was, and I was and am always on the right side of history. Now it was my job to prove I was always on the right side of history. Some force pulled me as I tried to stay back. I saw Geeta, Dirk, Linus, and Alala were all watching and trying to hold on to me like a human chain. My friends tried to keep us separated.

The magnetic force was too much as I flew and touched Maharani. My friends all came along with me like a chain and scattered all around. Her black band sealing her eyes completely vanished into thin air. She opened her eyes and there was a drop of a tear frozen in between her eye and her cheek. She kept her eyes frozen on me with shock, not how I saw Geeta look at Dirk. Her beautiful brown eyes gathered tears in them. The tears created a pool, but the water from the pool refused to overspill.

I heard a fearful screech come out of her mouth and freeze our whole home like an ice castle. She walked backward and stopped. She was shaking her head, right and left. She moved her hands up and down in disbelief. She tried to smell me and for a very short period of time, she was in shock. I assumed although she did smell me, her eyes betrayed her.

Her black hair flew with the help of the cold wind which was blowing in from the ocean through the open windows. Her eyes were getting overfilled as they started to pour out tears. The fallen tears were ready to take revenge.

Maharani said with a very trembling, cold, and shivering voice, “No, I don’t believe you. I watched you jump after my husband as I searched everywhere for him. I will rip this Earth apart to take revenge for the murder of my child and husband. What have you done with my husband, you monster? You killed him and my newborn child. You killed them both and so many others.”

Maharani stood frozen in place as she was blowing anger out of her ice queen body. She watched everyone in the room but kept glancing back at me. She then put her hair up in a bun.

She made a fist and said, “You fool, did you know I had twins? So, one of my boys still breathes through his future generations. You froze me in the past, but my child moved on. I won you fool. My boy's future generations will take revenge and hunt you down even if you remain a ghost. I will never ever forgive you and I promise I will hunt you to your last breath. You lost. You don't even realize it's not about immortality. It's about my love story being immortal."

I watched an emotionally hurt woman cry and tremble out of anger. She closed her eyes again and tried to reopen to only see my face staring at her. Her hair flew in the wind as her tears fell on the floor. I watched Linus catch her tears with his wings. Maharani saw Linus and tried to touch his face, but Linus flew outside after he caught her tears. Then, he flew back in but stood next to me. I thought he became invisible to her but was very visible to me.

The world was witnessing a dead woman's rage and anger which was born from pain and sorrow. I could sense an unjust storm was brewing within her. Even outside, everything became dark. Daytime became very dark and the bright sun pouring its light disappeared as we all witnessed darkness engulfed the land.

Screams from the islanders were heard even within the walls of the castle. The islanders were all running in different directions, trying to flee the island by jumping into the cold ocean and trying to swim to anywhere but here.

Everyone was witnessing all the events as all the doors and windows were ajar that allowed the castle to be a stage for the islanders.

Screams and cries were heard as everyone kept saying, "The witch is back! The gothic queen haunts our land and has eaten the sun. Darkness will never leave us. Why did we think she wouldn't get out of the castle or harm any one of us. She killed her father who was king and the prisoner who was hidden, only to rule this island. Now she can rule by beating death and becoming immortal."

I heard the words of fearful citizens as they all blamed me for purchasing this castle. They all had said to leave well enough alone and not to dig into the past as the past was lost and we only have the present for even the future is hidden in the wagon of time to only those who will be able to travel. People were all walking with a stick of fire in their hands.

I tried speaking to Maharani, "Please do not tremble out of anger, sweetheart, and sin. As then all you will have is resentment in your heart that you will carry around for eternity. Not everything is as it looks like as there is much more to every story."

She heard me loud and clear as she saw me with her big brown astonished eyes. She shook her head and placed her head backward. It was as if she could bend any way she wanted. Screams broke out even in my castle as now Maharani looked like a witch with a long silky black gown with intricate works on it. The gown touched the castle floors. Her long black hair fell out of the bun as her crown with nine jewels was sitting on her head. She tried to walk backward as she stopped herself trying to compose herself.

She was crying, and wiping her eyes and her nose as she made a fist. Then, she spread her hands outside of the castle as she cried and screamed. Her hands went to the ocean as she cried and was now grabbing herself with her hands.

She then said, "Why did you do this to me? I am the Queen of this land, and I curse you for you and your presence on this land, or any land you reside upon, because you my father had my sisters raped and witnessed the sin. You tried to have me raped. You murdered my son. Knowing everything and all the truth, this land and the citizens still worshiped you. Never did they ask for justice for the people. They say I their Queen am evil. I am their Queen through my husband. As you very well know, he was the King, not you, nor I, nor my sisters."

Maharani was watching over the land and ocean. I saw trees were falling. The land was filling up with ocean water that turned into blood. The ocean was being filled up with red smelly water that smelled like blood. I said nothing as I didn't want her to start harming people. That's when I would stop her.

She was watching everything she was doing and gave a shocking look as she said, "You murdered him for this castle, for me, and for everything here. You murdered him for this land, so I curse this land as even to this day, no one wants to find out the truth. They say I am evil. They say I killed you, I killed my husband, and that I killed my own child, all to be known as 'the Dead Queen.' What do you think is important to me?"

She was frantically crying as she rose, took a deep breath, and moved her hair from her eyes. She walked back closer to me as she said, "You, the citizens of this land, even to this day, still worship him. I curse you all to lose peace forever. You will find yourselves within disturbance, annoyance, fear, irritations, confusions, and a horror story that will never end until this face in front of me blows up and becomes ashes. I curse you tonight to always live in fear. Oh God, I must have some good deeds. Please let my deeds remove my father who was nothing but an evil monster. Let him become ashes to ashes, dust to dust."

From the castle and all over the island, everyone witnessed a horrific dance of blood-covered hands. From the deep ocean and its mystical blue water, a pair of hands appeared. The hands were covered with blood. The hands then flew above the island. The right hand went to the furthest right, and the left hand went to the furthest left. Then, we all witnessed blood pour over the island like a heavy rainfall. The holder of the hands wore a black dress that draped the floor. A huge crown with nine glowing moonstones spread light everywhere. It was like a forbidden mystery was going to be revealed.

Her long thick black hair draped beyond her knees. Her brown eyes were filled with anger and fair skin froze with sorrow. Her red lips trembled with agony. She just stood there looking over the island, trying to curse the island she lived within, where she had her sons, where she fell in eternal love, and where she wanted to write her romance novel.

I stood in front of a huge mirror that was behind Maharani as she was cursing and acting upon her curse. I refused to be terrorized or be cursed by the woman I loved and fought for until my last breath. Now awakened with my memories, I stood in front of her with the only face she detested. Yet she judged me because of my face. I wonder if her love for me was as pure as my love for her.

I stood by her even when everyone on the island said she was evil and a witch. I fought for her as my soul knew something was wrong. I laughed as I knew in the game of eternal love, vows, and promises, I kept mine. Yet she had broken hers by becoming a victim, then victimizing all on her path. The small quiet island by the ocean became loud as fearful bawls, cries, and panic spread across the land.

I stood in between her and the mirror. If only I could tell everyone not to fear her as she was afraid of everything that was happening to her. I watched people run in all different directions. I stood in between anger and the people of this land, the land I didn't know who owned in the past, but today is mine. I wouldn't allow her to ruin the people who worked and lived on the island by choice, not because they were imprisoned by a queen.

I held my breath and told my angry queen, "Hurt changes even the purest of souls, but I know I hold your love as a mirror of my love for you. Your curses won't touch me as my pure love for you will save me from your curses toward me. If you do murder me, historians will retell a love story where a wife searching for her beloved husband for a thousand years murdered him because she couldn't see the truth, nor recognize him. I only ask you to search your soul. Don't look at my face, but try to see my soul and find the answer to who am I."

WHO AM I

Oh,
My dearest,
The most feared,
The most dreaded
Beautiful queen
Roaming in the dark,
Why is it
I never feared you?
What is this magnet
We have
As I am pulled
Toward you?
I ask today,
Guide me
Toward the truth.
Show me
Not what
I fear,
But what and whom
You fear.
As
I ask not
Who you are,

But I ask you
To guide me
To seek,
Knock,
And ask
Your soul
To find out
The
Whole truth
About
WHO AM I.

Chapter Eight:

Soul To Soul

"From ashes
to ashes, dust
to dust, I call upon
you even after
death, as
true love and
lovers remain
immortal and are
tied in a knot from
soul to soul."

The sun was hidden behind the clouds as the islanders were all fleeing like an exodus. The sun and moon aligned while the Earth rotated and raised the water level. The high tide of the blue ocean reached land scientifically due to the moon's gravitational pull. Yet the islanders were saying the evil Dead Queen was angry, so she was flooding the land and everything on her path. People believed what they wanted to believe. Rarely did they stop to see what was in front of them, not what they thought was there. Even the Dead Queen saw what was in front of her eyes, not with the eyes of her soul.

I heard cries of a very hurt soul scream throughout the dark night. Neither did she hurt anyone, nor did she take her anger out on any person, being, or thing. She let out her painful cries and was asking her Creator to be just. Her cries, her pain, and her sufferings, people took as curses and spells. They all said she was trying to take the whole island down with her. Maybe when she was done, the island would cease to exist. Maybe it would go under the ocean and be buried like a memory.

All the castle windows were kept open to welcome the sweet breeze inside and eliminate all the negative air. Through the open windows, we heard one of the islanders yell, “The Dead Queen is back, and she will drown the island. Today, you see and know there is an island here. By morning, it will be missing. The existence of this island will be gone. No one will ever know there was an island here as the Dead Queen rises to take down the island with her into the ocean bed.”

From the open doors and windows, we witnessed elderly people running into canoes which were not safe to travel the big ocean. They were trying to escape the island.

Another islander screamed, “Was this land not his? Why is it called the Dead Queen’s Island and not the Imprisoned King’s Island?”

I looked outside and wondered what that mystery was about. The king’s island, not the queen’s? How many more mysteries would I have to face before this one mystery was solved? What were they saying about a king?

An elderly woman watched me through the opened walls as the mystical windows and doors allowed people to witness so many things in the castle. Maybe we should have closed these windows and doors. I needed privacy to deal with everything that was happening.

The woman with unkept hair and a frightened face was pointing her index finger at me, or I thought she was pointing at me as she said, “It’s all your fault. You had to buy the cursed castle. Why would you not first investigate this castle? It was the burial ground of the imprisoned King Lysandros. The Dead Queen's father, the castle knight, had murdered the King Lysandros and imprisoned his son somewhere in the castle before he took over the island. No one ever found out what happened to the son who was the real king, not the evil demonic witch. Maybe his body was buried in the castle walls."

I heard her, but I didn't know what she was talking about. It was then I saw Maharani standing behind me. I saw her within the mirrors of the magical rising phoenix's eyes. The phoenix was always there protecting me. It was full, not half, so I knew the twin flames were both watching over me. In the reflection, I saw Maharani had in her hand a shiny object. The sword pointing at me must have had the blood of so many innocents.

I speculated if the sword was the same object that had killed me in my last life. How did she have it? It was buried under the ocean with my lifeless body. How could I tell her revenge is not the way to any happily ever after, but through forgiveness. The words didn't leave my lips as I saw she was laughing like she was victorious.

Maharani watched my gaze as she laughed and said, "So Father, you do recognize the sword. Your sword you so preciously made and took with you to your grave. Yet dear Father, this is a replica I had made to murder you with if you ever return to my castle. Please know I hate you so much. I will not hesitate to take your life. I will do this slowly, so you suffer as much as I have suffered, as much as my Lysandros had suffered. You brutally murdered his whole family. You took over his castle and his inheritance. You had imprisoned him for life. The prince never knew his own identity or how he was the king and not a criminal. You imprisoned him to take his crown and declared yourself the false king. I will take revenge, I promise!"

Suddenly, a sharp pain shot down my knees as I watched the sword barely touch my skin. From out of the blue, I saw a mirror appeared and protected me from feeling the full brunt of the sword. The mirror had the following words flashing, "MIRROR OF TWIN FLAMES: Twin flames are made from one another for one another. Never shall they be able to harm one another even if one fails to recognize the other."

I only hoped the Dead Queen would give up her anger for a few seconds to see things around her. The angry queen saw nothing, but her anger spilled out into the cold night as she cried again and screamed for her beloved husband. She wanted to kill me with her bare hands in anger for her dead husband. The beast was laughing somewhere out in the deep ocean.

I heard him say, "Come on Maharani, finish him up. He is evil for I am coming, and I still live just like you. I am on the same land where you live, not with the living, but the dead. It is better to kill and remove all those we do not like and those who have ruined us."

Maharani was crying and screaming at the same time. It seemed like she was blindfolded through her sorrows as her soul saw nothing but the unjust done to her husband. I didn't know if she existed anymore as within her soul there was only her husband. How could I tell her not to love me so much that you forget yourself and everything around you.

Maharani asked, "Is that you Lysandros? How has death changed you? I loved you because you taught me to only love and not harm or take revenge. I never imagined you would change. Even after being wronged, you forgave all and tried to teach me to forgive. But what are you saying now?"

Maharani was crying as she wiped her tears that were freezing when they fell, and then said, "Who is scaring the islanders and spreading blood and fear all around? I have not but then who has? Where are you Lysandros? I still wear the black dress as I eternally honor our union and want the world here underneath the Earth, on the Earth, and above in the skies to know I am a widow. You broke your promise by dying and leaving me behind."

I stood watching her and the island which was facing a devastation. There was a tsunami going on as houses and resort shops were all being damaged by this unexpected storm.

Maharani then again said, "How cursed am I that I cannot even die properly and be with you? I hate you Lysandros so much that I only fear what I will do with my hatred. This monster has taken your name and stands in front of me saying you have been reborn with this monster's face. Why would you do this to me and take the face of my father who tried to get me raped by his goons? His goons had more decency as they did not want to touch a pregnant woman, so they fibbed to their boss and saved my honor."

Then I saw Maharani bend and fall to the ground repeating my name as she cried and screamed. This screaming continued as no one had the courage to talk to the Dead Queen who at any moment might just get up and throw us out. As I watched her scream and cry, it was the worst situation as I could do nothing but watch the love of my eternity collapse even after death. She stood up and tried to gather herself. Stones and arrows made from iron with fire burning on them flew into the castle toward Maharani.

I stood in front of them as I shouted and told everyone, “Stop it! In the name of love, with love, and for love, please stop it. Do not do unjust to her as she is doing unjust to you. She is lost in her land of love. Just look! She is devastated because of her dead husband. She is grieving his loss. She is not dressed in black because she is a demoness, but because she is a widow. Please! Do not hurt her!”

Maharani just stood there and didn’t try to see or hear anything. A very hurt woman stood in front of me not hiding her pain or fear as she knew she was a ghost and had been trapped here for a long, long time. She shed tears that could have made rivers and canals. She sang songs that could have made thousands of blockbusters. Yet all her tears and songs washed away through the river of time that had changed its course.

So many people were born and had died in between. So many more love stories were written, yet Maharani’s love story never found a page in the diaries of history, nor did her sad songs find a singer. Her tears washed away everything as if nothing ever existed other than a fearful woman who frightened away all who came near her.

She put her hands together and through the open windows, she looked up toward the Heavenly skies and pleaded with a broken voice, "I ask You, my Creator, how is all this fair in Your eyes? You bring in front of me the person who ruined my sisters, my mother, my stepmothers, and murdered my husband. Now You want me to believe he is my Lysandros? I ask You, oh my God, have mercy and do tell me how much more am I going to be punished for sins I may have committed but are still unknown to me. Like I said maybe a thousand years ago, I will never call You nor will I shed tears for You my God, as I will take this as a punishment You give to even the innocent. Yet I pray please don't punish my Lysandros and give him the face of the man even Heavens above will fear to see."

She saw me as the moon's glow shined into my room. We had lost electricity. I knew this island had trouble with electricity, so power outages were normal. Everyone who still lived on the island was very well equipped with fuel-burning lanterns and generators. The island was heavily leaning on solar power. The whole castle was shining with candles and lanterns. Just like the whole day, the night remained the same and we were heavily covered in darkness. People were saying it was the end of time as day and night were the same. Everywhere eyes could see was completely dark.

We only knew the day had ended as our watches told us so. Even in the dark, I could see in front of me stood the ghost of a dead woman, dressed all in black. Even though she scared the wit out of everyone, I didn't fear her. She could come to me in any form, and I knew my heart belonged to only her.

I wanted to comfort her, not be the reason of her discomfort. I knew I had to wait out the time neither she had nor did I. There was a huge crown that graced her head like it was probably glued onto her head. Her big brown eyes were staring at me. She had no wish to live or fight for anything. She was a woman who faced death and loss at the same time. I knew all my love for her would not bring her back to me as I was living with a face, she blamed all her tragedies on.

I told her, "I don't blame you. I hate myself too. I hate my face and wonder why God would separate us repeatedly. Please do as you wish and end the story now. Maybe in death, I will regain my face. Then, you will believe me, that I am Lysandros, not your father. Before you leave, tell the world that love stories are based on faces, not souls.

My dear, let the world know eternal love does not exist. Only facial love exists."

Within the guest room where I was living, there was a crowd. Linus and Alala walked in through the small hand-carved doors. They leaned against floor-to-ceiling bookcases made out of metal and iron. Geeta and Dirk too rushed in and sat on the bedroom bench by the foot of the bed. They were all watching this drama take place in front of everyone's eyes. Maharani walked with grace. She stood in front of me as she raised her sword to my face. She had no guilt or sympathy for the holder of this face.

She said with authority, "King Villainous, how does it feel to be back in a human body? Do you in this life have a male part? In your last life, remember you did not. Your mother cut it off when you tried to rape her. You were evil even as a child. So, you lived behind a cloak of lies."

Geeta laughed as she placed a hand on her face in shock. Alala looked at Geeta and gave her the "I told you so" look. I hoped my furious queen didn't get too annoyed at my girls. If she tried to hurt Geeta or Alala, I would get in between. Even in a love story, there is a limit to where wrong is wrong and right is right. As Maharani watched the girls, I stood in between them.

Maharani laughed at everyone, then she said directly at me, “You could not produce so you captured men to produce with your wives. Then, you murdered your wives and the men so no proof would remain that your children were not your biological children. Later, you murdered your own children, so no one could talk. What about Lysandros? What about his parents whom you killed to take over the castle? Why did you do all this? Why did you live your whole life buried inside of a lie? You wonder how Lysandros escaped your prison? That was the only secret that bothered you all your life.”

She watched me with so much hatred, I felt so let down. All my life of waiting for her faded and burned out like ashes. The woman everyone on the island feared and I loved with all my soul just washed away all my love with dirty words that had no place within my soul. I only hoped she didn’t with bitter words separate the souls of twin flames.

Anger replaced my sadness and at times, I had to bite my lips and make a fist as to control my hatred toward myself. Sweetheart, if only you knew how much I hate myself. I stood on my two feet, yet it felt like I was standing on quicksand. The Earth beneath was shaking my belief in true love. I wanted to be strong and steady. How could I rip out my soul and show the other half of my soul that I too had been waiting for a thousand years.

I too asked my Creator questions and like whispers, my words came out, "Why my God, do I have his face? I know he did some kind of magic under the ocean. When he killed me, he too drowned. As we were both drowning, he said something, and our faces switched. He got only my face as I got his. Our bodies did not switch. Now You, my God, tell me how all this is even possible. I would never ask a woman to fall in love with a man who has her father's face, even if her father was the most innocent soul on Earth. Not in this life, but maybe in another. As you waited for me for a thousand years, I too will wait for you for even more."

Maharani watched me as she at first looked like she was in shock. Then, she laughed and shook her head. She walked out of the room and just disappeared into thin air. The room felt cold and somewhat eerie. I thought it would be eerie with a ghost inside of a room, not when the ghost left.

I saw Linus was walking back and forth with his wings lifted, creating air pressure like he was ready to fly. Maybe this was his defense mechanism, or maybe he was getting ready to protect someone. My thoughts could not have come sooner as I watched a sword not ghostly but real sword come flying to my heart. It froze in thin air as I heard a chant of words floating in the middle of the room. The words came out of a puddle of water that created a mirror in front of me.

The words were floating in the air as they were recited by themselves and said, "Twin flames are born for one another, separated in life and death to find oneself yet only complete when they unite. Twin flames are protected by the water of life and death from murdering one another. If one is alive, then both have a chance to be back. If one is murdered at the hand of the other, then never shall you two unite but become ashes."

I saw my soul was ripping out of my body as was hers. We both watched two halves of a phoenix were flying. I knew I was one half, and the other half was Maharani. I felt my heart was throbbing as I saw the sword come and shatter the glass that was in front of me. As the sword came toward my chest, Linus and Alala with their wings held on to the sword.

The sword then went backward and was going toward Maharani's heart. I wondered how the sword could harm a dead woman's body. Then as I realized, like a bolt of lightning, I ripped my hands through the magical ocean of life and death and through the mirror of life and death. With all my might, I pushed the sword toward the ceiling. I saw my soul in the form of a phoenix enter my body. The other half of the same bird entered Maharani's ghostly dead body.

The mirror made from a material like water disappeared as did the two halves of the phoenix. The sword went back to the woman who threw it. She dropped the sword on the ground as she fell to the ground and cried. I wanted to break the fall and catch her, yet I knew I couldn't as she was a ghost, and I was still a human.

I saw Linus and Alala fly outside as the doors to the back veranda was ajar. The veranda was supported by cast iron and steel. There was a lot of woodwork imitating stone carvings I had never seen before. Flowering plants including the Queen of the Night, star jasmine, and the night-blooming jasmine, mixed their amazing fragrances and sent out a message, even in the dark fearful night, that night-blooming flowers were there to give all hope. The twinkling stars were shining in the skies reminding the dead are not gone for they keep an eye out for their loved ones. Yes, the deadly beast too roamed around in the form of a man or a beast or maybe a friend for revenge, yet I've always believed where there is hope, there is a way.

I vowed, my beloved, to find a way out of the deep dark ocean to unite with you, dead or alive. I was yours and shall always be yours. I could teach you to let go of your anger and burn it to ashes. Forgiveness is much more powerful than revenge. I could guide you through this in good time.

The truth haunted me as I knew all dead must return to their Creator through the tunnel of light. I promised my beloved, I would wait for her eternally for our union if not in this life, then in another. Love stories end in marriages, so somehow, I wanted to get to the end of our love story. Memories have told me our love story began with our marriage but did not last to find our happily ever after.

Wedding vows from another lifetime never faded nor were they forgotten. This beloved groom of yours solemnly swore to find the truth, the complete truth, with my God's help, as my promise to you, from soul to soul.

SOUL TO SOUL

Oh,
My love,
My beloved wife,
Yes,
I do remember.
Yes,
I do treasure.
Yes,
I said
With our wedding vows,
Not in this life
But in another.
Memories I hold
Safely
Within my soul.
I will
Always honor,
Always love,
And always be true to
Only you.
I promise
I will never forget
Our love story

That held us in union
As twin flames from
SOUL TO SOUL.

Chapter Nine:

Heart Beats Or Not

"If ever
separated, oh
beloved of mine,
find me in
the skies,
under the
ocean, and
beyond the Earth
even if my heart
beats or not."

The morning sun never appeared as darkness filled the skies. We knew it was morning as our phones and electronic devices told us so. The skies were dark and even the stars were missing. It felt like our land was suffocating, as if someone was holding this island in prison tied under a black cloak. There wasn't much breathing space between homes. Each home had lanterns burning.

The people who still remained on the island were all too scared to come out of their homes. Reporters were trying to get to the island from all over the world. They wanted to report on the Dead Queen who was haunting the island and who was holding all the inhabitants as prisoners. Boats trying to leave with people circled and came back to the island. Not a single person could leave.

Children were crying in fear as adults were trying to calm them down. Food was being rationed as were other needed supplies. The electricity was still gone. All the phone lines and cable services were down. The whole island was being held prisoner in a dungeon by the beast, whom people feared, and thought was the Dead Queen.

Tasmanian devils were screeching and hunting for food. Nocturnal animals couldn't tell if it was day or night, or even if they could, they wanted to hunt. Children were being kept inside. Dingoes were also howling like prowling wolves in open air. These animals generally avoided humans. I wondered if the hunted animals thought the humans were in danger so they could become the hunters and the humans could be the hunted. For me, it wasn't what I couldn't see but what I could see that became the danger I had to deal with.

The captain of my ship and friend Dirk sat next to me on the veranda as he said, "Do something. Maybe tell her you are sorry and let her walk through the light. Maybe then, the light in our lives too will be back. If she really loved you or loves you, then why would she let your people and loved ones suffer?"

Dirk let his hair fly in the wind. His shirt was left untucked as he sat next to me barefoot. It was like everyone in our household became so jittery, we forgot if we had shoes on, or if we were in our pajamas or loungewear or outdoor clothes.

He then said, "I get it. You have her evil father's face. The islanders don't have her father's face. They're not related to him. So, why are they being punished? Seriously, this is too much. Tell her to stop or do something before we all disappear into the dark. Or maybe we will become that island which never existed and only can be found in books.

Mothers will tell their children to finish their food or Uncle Dirk will appear from the Dead Queen's Island."

Before I could say anything we all saw Maharani was just standing there. She wiped her eyes and walked closer to the edge of the balcony.

Dirk got up and said, "Be careful! The railings are not safely secured!"

The woman had no humor in her as she listened to him and didn't even flinch an inch. She walked to the railing and stood on top of it in the air. She watched Dirk and he watched her. She gave him a look and just did what she wanted to do.

He then said, "Oops, sorry dead woman. I forgot you're already dead. So, no worries there. It's just that we the living are in trouble. Why would you care? You don't have a heart that beats."

She gazed at Dirk as if could see inside him. She did nothing but kept walking in the air. Her hair became longer and longer as she told all of us to be quiet by placing a finger on her lips. There was a lightning bolt from nowhere lighting up the skies. Then, darkness poured over the land again. I watched the ghost woman who was feared by all extend her hands. Her arms were getting longer and longer. She placed her hands in the water, and she picked up a huge crocodile, which wasn't common in this area. Crocodiles are normally found in northern Australia.

The crocodile was hissing and growling. It turned repeatedly. Then, the crocodile was dropped on the veranda in front of us. None of us shrieked or moved. Linus and Alala stayed inside the huge bedroom I was using as my personal bedroom off the veranda. I needed a bedroom with a study to finish my book. So, I chose that room rather than the original master bedroom.

Alala and Linus held on to one another as we all saw a phoenix flying over the castle. At all times, the phoenix had its fireball eyes on the castle. It became huge with an orange and red glow. The wings looked like they were made of fire. They were so colorful that they mesmerized all who saw them.

Maharani tied a leash made from an iron rod to hold the crocodile. The reptile was now trembling as it growled and wanted to go back to the ocean where it could hunt down all things he chose.

Maharani said, "Show yourself in front of us. Who are you? Why are you placing spells on my land? You covered up the sun and now all the people of this land think it is end of time. You have been harming my people and I will not allow you to do so by any means. All the blood and tsunamis you have been creating and blaming me like always. That is fine, but why harm innocents who are not involved?"

Maharani tied the crocodile with her fingers and held on to it. She was trying to see him, inspecting it closely.

She then said, "As the Queen of this land, I will not tolerate any harm to befall them. I can say whatever I want to them, but how could I harm my husband's people, his land, and his kind? I cannot tolerate any harm done on him or to ruin his name. It is I who was providing for them for a thousand years. It is I who watched over them and made sure they were always safe."

The beast laughed and then went missing. Somehow, it disappeared. Then, I saw the reptile on the cliff below the castle. In front of us, the reptile became Linus or someone who looked like Linus. The eyes, however, betrayed him. Linus's warm-hearted soul was missing. In his form stood a man who was demonic. His eyes kept changing and his mouth kept hissing.

He gave me a look and I knew this was the fake Linus. Maharani pulled him back by his iron chain collar. That's when I saw a man in agony just stand in front of us. The reptile was gone. I never thought in my entire life I would get to see a reptile become a man. Yet I knew in this dark world, it's the dead humans who are beginning to take forms of animals or other humans.

The man who looked like my incarnation from last life stood in front of us. He saw Maharani who watched him without blinking. Tears rolled from her eyes. She forgot to blink or move. My inner soul hurt more than words could ever express. I was forced to witness my beloved fall prey and cry for me yet only at the sight of a man who looked like my last life's form.

Her tears fell on the ground as my eyes too felt her pain. I couldn't stop the tears from falling as I knew I was fighting a losing battle. A ghost was crying for a ghost, and here I was a mere man with a mortal body. For me, the battle wasn't about winning. I only wanted my beloved to be safe in Heaven or on Earth. I didn't want her to be stuck in purgatory or Hell by being trapped in this dungeon for so long.

I spoke out loud as I said, "For my love for you, I will set you free as you deserve to be in Heaven, not in Hell."

Maharani turned toward me as I saw the hatred in her eyes. I cared not for her hatred or her anger as my love for her was eternal. All I wanted was for her to be safe.

I remembered a verse we had recited when we were together for the first time. Like flashes, the words came flying back to me as I recited to my beloved, our song. We had taken a vow to remember, wait, and never stop loving one another even when our heart beats or not.

HEART BEATS OR NOT

Forgive me,
Forgive me,
Forgive me,
Dear God,
Forgive me
As I love my beloved
More than I love
My heartbeats,
My mind,
My body,
Or my soul.
Dear God,
Forgive me
As I see my beloved
In the air,
In the skies,
In the ocean,
In the flowers,
And on the land.
I smell her
Even within the breeze
Like sweet passionate kisses
Blowing toward me.

I only see my beloved
Everywhere,
Anywhere,
Ubiquitously,
As I bow down
To my beloved,
Our love,
And our union.
In life or in death,
I pray
Our love story
Be written
From soul to soul
Throughout time,
Throughout all generations,
Even a thousand years later,
Even when
My
HEART BEATS OR NOT.

Chapter Ten:

Separated By A Heartbeat

"Twin flames
rise from the ashes
with one another.
Then how is it
here I have
risen and you
have not for we
are separated
by a
heartbeat."

The veranda became a fear retreat where everyone held their breath. The skies kept silent as they knew two lovers were trying to find one another in the dark. So, the skies even kept the moon hidden as they knew the only glow that was allowed was from the twin flames glowing for one another.

The Earth was calm and quiet as she too realized thousands of days, thousands of nights, and a thousand years have passed since two lovers saw one another. So, she too asked her trees, her birds, and prowling night creatures to keep quiet. The darkness that engulfed the small island didn't come in between as the glow from our souls burned the darkness.

We both saw a mirror appear from the crown. I saw the mirror, but my mind kept asking what I was scared of. It was strange how life's events separated my twin flame from me. I never thought I would have to live without her. The pain of separation ripped out all my solace and calmness.

Not being recognized by my own twin flame was even worse than being separated from her. In separation, I had my sweet dreams and my memories. When my eyes fell on her eyes and I only saw rejection not recognition as she kept herself in prison, then I wondered if separation was better than rejection.

My beloved, I would place all my feelings within the confinement of my inner soul. I've loved you more than I could ever hate you. You had said if I was the sky, you would appear as a star. If I was the ocean, you would appear as a starfish. If I was the green grass, you would appear as a wildflower. Yet here as God gave me a face that you hate, you became the person who wished to end my life.

The mysterious mirror stood in between us. In the mirror like a miracle, Maharani saw me and saw my face from a thousand years ago which was captured by a demonic creature. The demonic creature that she placed a rope around stood behind her. She saw its reflection in the mirror. It had a face like mine but different as it had no love, no feelings, and no care but only abhorrence toward everything.

The mirror was like a digital photo frame which played a video of the underwater face switching. Watching the video, I had to live through the horrific nightmare again. To top it off, I was living with a face that resembled the demon. We saw how King Villainous and I were fighting under water. As my body turned cold and breathless, my heart stopped playing any beats and all the music in my life became quiet and dark. The demonic king whispered a rhyme.

We saw a bolt of lightning hit us both as my face became like his and his face became like mine. Our souls were not switched. We both had no heartbeats as I felt his cold body became lifeless like mine. I went down to the ocean floor. King Villainous rose above the water heartless and beatless. He was a dead man who walked the grounds of Earth with my face, which by the way looked so much like Linus yet again different. He screamed as he realized his spell only worked for the face, not with the rest of the body. From under the water, my dead baby boy rose and gave me the light I needed.

As time went on, I saw my dead twin son's soul entered my other son's body and both became one. As I went to the tunnel of reincarnation, my boys went with me and became my best buddy Linus. For that reason, we were born from the same place together to be with one another. Linus even in death did not die as he became the eternal phoenix who was much more powerful dead than alive.

Maharani walked closer to me as I saw the mirror float away and disappear. King Villainous walked closer to us as he smirked and touched his daughter. If I could with my bare hands, I would take a chance to throw him to Hell for his punishments to begin. Yet I knew it was all my God's will, not mine. So, I kept faith alive.

King Villainous said, "Sweetheart you have my crown. I would like to have it back. You loved this face, so why walk backward? I have been blessed to have a face that you so much loved. Do you understand your beloved is still in the world of the living? He reincarnated but you did not. So, let me help you get rid of him and all his people. That way, you would appreciate my gift as then both of you would be in the land of the dead."

Maharani screamed, "Please my God, save my twin flame and all his people, his land, his home, and his family. I have not sinned knowingly, but I was born to evil. Do not punish me anymore by making me watch my beloved suffer. Love is blind, love is pure, love is innocent, and love heals everything."

She stood in between King Villainous and me. She placed her hands together and prayed for guidance and help from Heavens above. She lowered her head and kept her hands in a praying position.

Maharani continued, "So, with my pure love for my twin flame, I ask You, my God, be merciful and grant him safety, protection, and all the happiness of the world. I will take for him all the sorrows, all the tears, all the unhappiness, and disappear to purgatory, or to Hell. Maybe with this prayer in the name of the Father, the Son, and the Holy Spirit, as I seek salvation through the triune God, I will be saved and will go to Heaven if You my Lord accept my prayers."

I saw the mirror above came down as it was pouring water. The demonic King Villainous was suddenly screaming in pain. He was burning from the water touching him. We all watched in shock how a man standing on the veranda was burning from water being poured onto him from within the mirror.

Geeta screamed, "Holy water! As a Hindu, it's like Ganges water. It burns evil. He is being burned down by a prayer recited from the soul of an innocent for another innocent soul. It is holy water through all faiths."

I felt weird as I heard King Villainous scream and ask for help. He was mind playing everyone as I saw my friend Linus screaming for help. I almost ran, but as I tried to move and help him, I found myself in a mirror where I couldn't move.

I yelled and said, "It's Linus, my best friend! My brother, please let me save him, even if it means I must die! Please someone help me. Oh God, buddy, how could I live if you are no more? Please let me try to save you."

Above us the magical phoenix flew as Linus and Alala came and stood in union, then as individuals. They poured tears on top of King Villainous. Linus looked at me and signaled to me it's not him. After all the inflicted pain, I just let my tears roll out. I did not hide my tears. Nor did I secretly wipe them. Maybe it would lessen the pain, the hurt, and the loss.

Linus said directly to King Villainous, "You murdered your three daughters, your son-in-law, your wives, numerous other women, men, and your daughter's son. Yes, I am here because you forgot to kill the surviving son whom my forefathers raised as their own. My twin brother you had killed became a phoenix and we became one in our incarnation. Your own mother was killed at your hands because you knew she was the first witness to your brutality. You, the lowest of all low, a demon, had raped your own mother. She was successful in chopping of your genitals before she died. Her dying curse to you for eternity was, never shall you touch another woman or become a father."

Linus walked directly next to King Villainous, now half-man and half-water. Linus didn't fear the evil man who was still laughing and not scared of what was happening. He was laughing nonstop like he was intoxicated with laughing gas or something. He saw me and Maharani directly as he wanted to do something again. I saw he was murmuring a spell. Alala stood in front of me with a very stern face.

Biting her lips and cringing her eyes, Alala said, "No evil man! You won't whisper any spells for nothing will work. Lysandros is protected through the love of his twin flame. Whatever face or form he takes, his twin flame will recognize him as they are half of one whole. You can't do anything by switching faces. Your soul is demonic, and you shall enter the boat of the Grim Reaper who waits for you."

It was then like the thunder roaring, we all heard King Villainous scream in fear. He was now crying and looking at Maharani. He tried to utter words and convince her he was Lysandros and everything everyone was saying was false. He screamed with a stone face.

Shaking and trembling, he said, "Maharani, please look at me. Do you think this face is evil? I am Lysandros, so please forgive me and save me. We both are on the same land. Maybe we can be together or even go to purgatory together. I know how to escape from there. Just come with me. Give me your hands please."

We were all standing with fear on the veranda, wondering what to do next. We heard a voice humming. Then, we heard from far away a song was playing. It seemed like from within the ocean, a man was singing. He was rowing a boat. His hand was busy pushing the rough ocean waters with his oars. He had on a black robe with a hood. On his boat, he had a lantern that was half burning, yet the glow was so powerful that it brightened everything around us.

The song that was being heard from all over the island said the same line repeatedly,

"I have traveled for you.
I have waited for you.
I have heard your tales
Of destruction,
Of dishonesty,
And your unjust rulings.
After dawn comes darkness,
So now I the Grim Reaper
Have come for you.
You must travel
To the land of judgment
As I am here especially for you."

Suddenly, King Villainous floated over the railings of the veranda, then over the huge boulders, bumping into each rock, as he slowly went toward the boat.

He was screaming and crying as he was staring with a sinister look and said, "I bought myself immortality. I was given a gold coin by you who said to wish for what I wanted, and I wished for immortality. You can't take me away!"

The Grim Reaper stood on the water as he floated above and took King Villainous in his hands like a small puppet.

He smiled, gave an ominous look, and said, "Foolish mortal, I never gave you anything. The only time I meet anyone is at the end of their life. You became the fallen and hid in the shadows of the lost souls, yet everyone who is lost will be found when and if I want to find you. I want you to take a journey with me, so let's get going or I will take you by force."

The boat of the Grim Reaper left in a smoke. The water mirror too disappeared.

Maharani walked to the edge of the ocean with tears in her eyes and quivering lips as she said, "Oh Grim Reaper, what plans do you have for me? I did not run away from death or life as I never had a chance to live or die within my wish. Everything was decided for me. The only thing I wished was for Lysandros to be my husband as I know we are twin flames. I cannot stop loving him because I am dead, and he is alive. Please come and take me on my boat of death. I wait for you. I never hid for until a few days ago, I did not realize I was dead."

The Grim Reaper did not reply to her, or if he did, we didn't hear anything. The darkness evaporated as daylight peeked through into our island. I walked outside into the courtyard as I saw the islanders were all going on with their lives. Something peculiar just happened and no one even cared. It all seemed unreal.

I walked under the covered area of the veranda and saw Maharani, Linus, and Alala were conversing. I walked next to Dirk and Geeta as they were like me shaking with fear, fury, and confusion. Geeta, Dirk, and I loved to stand on the uncovered part of the veranda as that gave us a feeling somehow, we were closer to the ocean. I didn't know if we would love the ocean as much anymore though.

Linus closed his eyes, took a deep breath, and remained quiet for a while. Then, with a grief-stricken and emotional face, he said, "The islanders won't remember anything. All they will remember is a tsunami warning was issued and the whole island needed to be evacuated. The evacuation is being handled as we speak. The whole evacuation process will take up to three days. I knew something was happening up in the Heavens, but I didn't know what. Maybe the whole island would disappear and go under water."

Maharani stood on the veranda and was watching the blue ocean. I walked outside and joined her. Without waiting for her to say anything, I asked her, "Why and how did we fall in love? I don't remember anything beyond our marriage. Why did you fall for a pauper if your father, a king, never would have given his blessings? Another question off topic or on topic, why did you darken the island for three days?"

Maharani looked at me in astonishment as she was either confused or smiling in her own thoughts. I could not say what she thought. She looked upset yet very quickly changed her emotion and sat across me not next to me so she could see me clearly.

She said very swiftly and without any hesitation, "You really forgot how we fell in love? Reincarnation does that? Here I thought after death I have been slowly forgetting everything. I did not darken the island. I was blind for all these years until as it was foretold, my twin flame would enter the castle and touch me. Only then, would I regain my sight. So, I knew it was you, yet your face got in between. I tried to see you blindfolded and yes, I felt you. Yet the memories of his face freaked me out. I know he was behind everything. I wish I knew how he did that. I don't as for me days go by, and I forget everything but the memory of losing you never faded."

She stopped and walked to the rose garden off the veranda. She tried to smell the roses but with her hand gestured nothing. She couldn't smell anything. Yet I wondered how she could still smell me. I didn't ask as I knew the answer. It's like I could smell her even when I didn't know who she was. All these years I refused to date or even go out with any other woman. I knew she existed, somewhere in this universe. Little did I know we were separated by just one heartbeat.

She silently indicated for me to follow her. There my two guardian angels Linus and Alala showed up. I heard footsteps of Dirk and Geeta running after me.

We all stopped in front of a side wall that was covered in bushes. Huge trees grew covering the wall and giving the impression that no one had ever come here. Maharani signaled Linus to do something. There as Linus lifted his wings, the trees were gone, and a gatelike prison appeared in front of us. The grills opened as I jumped into the past.

I was a child and cried in fear of the cold. A girl appeared as she gave me blankets and bread and cheese. She tried to take off my shackles, but they were stuck to my hands. An old man came now and then as he changed the shackles, gave me food, and left. The shackles were long so I could use the bathroom and eat and sleep. Yet no sign of daylight ever entered the prison.

The girl with panic in her voice said, "My father with his goons murdered your father, the king of the island. Your mother was murdered and now my father has called himself the king of the island. He said you will be in prison forever as your father had special powers unlike a human but like a warlock or something. I will try to listen and give you the details."

I watched days go by as the girl became Maharani and I was a grown-up man in prison. Everyone forgot about me but her. She never gave up trying to cut my shackles, but we both decided they were magical. One day as Maharani was very sick and was beaten for trying to come and see me, she sent a message to me with an old man.

The old man came to the prison and bowed down in front of me, saying, "Your Highness, forgive me. I was not involved in what had happened to you. As both your parents were murdered, we all believed you were murdered with them. This man is evil, and he can do magic spells. He has murdered his wives and removes them from Earth just with a spell. He is a demon, yet I will set you free with the only wand your father the king of this land left me with. This sword he said was magic and to use it once only when you need it. I have waited for years but the demon erases my memories."

It was then just by raising the sword, my shackles were all gone. The old man showed me the way to Maharani's room. He also gave me change of clothes and a bag my father had left behind. I changed my clothing and walked into the castle with my bag.

As I met King Villainous, I told him, "I wish to cure your daughter with my magic if you promise to give her hand in marriage to me. In return, I will give you what you ask for."

The wind blew into the castle as I saw people were all whispering, "A magician is here. He said he can wake up the princess and will marry her. He is stronger than the king!"

The small island was crowded as people from all over wanted to see the magician and ask for something. Yet King Villainous wanted me all for himself as he forced me to his castle.

King Villainous looked at me and said, "So, what if I tell you she is dead and if you can bring her back to life, I will want you to grant me eternal life? Even after death, I want to rule this island."

I placed my hands in the bag and wondered was my father really a magician of some kind? Even I can at times, extend my hands or see things beyond water and Earth. Only the heavy weighted iron chain could keep me locked up. Nothing made sense but I just stood there thinking how evil and greedy could a person be, that he wants to rule for eternity?

Without thinking as I saw the people in the castle were all saying the princess is no more, I said, "So we have a deal."

I walked upstairs and saw my princess was cold and had no heartbeats. I kissed her lips and told her mind to mind, "Beautiful princess, don't leave me as I am still alive. How could you leave me and not even give me one lifetime together? I have given up my immortality to have one lifetime with you. Yes, I am different. My parents gave up their immortality to keep me alive. I have given this up to your father to keep you alive."

Maharani woke up and stood in front of me. She hugged me and I held on to her.

King Villainous walked in and laughed as he said, "Give me the bag and get out of here with that woman. I don't want to feed another mouth if I don't have to. Also, remember, you said I get your father's immortality."

We left the castle and were happy to have one life to live together, as husband and wife. We were left alone for a long time until we were both captured and taken back to the castle. Our married life did not last long as evil eyes fell upon our union. Even after giving up immortality, I could not have one simple life to live with my beloved.

Then, I saw we were in the chambers of the evil king, who stole my throne and my crown, as he now wanted to have my family's immortality. We walked into the huge room which smelled foul, like so much sin and unjust happened here. I tried to remember my father and mother yet could not. On the wall was my portrait drawn on the stone walls. Someone tried to whitewash it out, but could not as it appeared all over again. I realized I was looking at King Lysandros, not me but my father.

King Villainous looked at me and was visibly upset at my inspection of my father's portrait which he failed to remove. He looked sick and furious as he shouted at me and said, "Did you know I can't have the immortality until you die, as through death, your father gave it to you. Now I must kill you to get my immortality."

Everything changed again as I was being thrown from one spot to another.

I asked my beloved and Linus, "Please both of you go slowly. These changes of sceneries are making me dizzy and very nauseous."

Suddenly again, I was under the ocean drowning as I saw the evil demonic king was trying to murder me. The ruthless and heartless demonic person did not care for or about anyone else, but himself.

He said, "You don't have immortality, so now drown and I will take everything you have and even your face as you can have mine. Now switch."

As I was drowning, I remembered the immortality switches from father to son at the son's birth, so I said, "I give the immortality to my living son. For eternity, may you have immortality. If you are a human or a bird or any form you so choose, may you have this power and may your twin flame, have it too. For I have given this up to be with my twin flame dead or alive."

I had no feelings as everything seemed to be dimming. My entire being felt like I did not exist anymore, yet I gathered enough strength to pray.

So, I prayed and said, "Villainous, whether you be immortal or not, this power for you won't be eternal. It is only until the Grim Reaper so chooses you to be or not be. Who am I to give you anything? So, let my Creator do as He so wishes. I have passed everything I was gifted by my forefathers to my only living son."

I jumped back to the present times as I saw everyone around me was all wet. Everyone went with me to my past through my memories. Yet somehow it felt like we were all there. I watched Linus as we hugged and I told him, "May my prayers and our forefathers' gifts be with you eternally."

Maharani was crying and said, "Why did you give up immortality to become a human only to die and not even spend one lifetime with me? How was it fair? You kept your promise, and he broke his, yet we were separated through the hands of a demon. For a thousand years, I have been praying to my God, my Creator, for justice, to be able to have you my husband as my partner in life and in death. Maybe my sin was my vows did not say till death do us apart, but in all my rebirths and even after death."

I tried to hold her, just hug her once. Physical relationship to me was from soul to soul. Just knowing how much I love her, and she loves me was enough to last for eternity. Sweetheart, just one kiss would have kept me going even more. I knew it wasn't possible as in between us we had such a distance. I couldn't catch up even if I was breathless, as you are breathless by one heartbeat. Just one heartbeat apart, yet still my heart beats eternally your name.

I tried to see her through my tears. I realized even our eyes became foggy and we were not able to see one another clearly because of the fog we created for one another through running tears. Why did tears roll nonstop even though I had told my tears not to fall anymore? Why did my heartbeats call her name when she didn't have any heartbeats at all? My God, why have You punished her for loving me and punished me by separating her from me?

I watched Linus and Alala and told everyone, "I am sorry everyone. My heartbeats have betrayed me as I fell in love and did what I had to only to be with my beloved wife. Yet Linus, I am blessed to know I was able to transfer this blessing to you and Alala. Until your children are of age, you two decide how to keep this blessing going."

Maharani watched me with her tear-filled eyes. She saw Linus and gave him an air hug. I realized she was scared to hug him in case she burned him by hugging. It was so strange as even her tears kept freezing, and I knew it was painful to even cry. She kept turning her head to hide her pain. She always suffered but never let me feel the pain. The world called her demonic, evil, and the Dead Queen, yet I knew she only fell in love with me. She was the innocent wife who suffered unjustly not just at the hands of the demonic king, but the world and all the unjust mouths of the unjust.

My beloved's hair flew in the wind as I could smell her natural scent. Her satin and silk combined dress dragged on the ground as she honored my death from last life and kept our love story alive by dressing as a widow. Yet the unjust people thought she was a demonic witch because she wore black.

I saw she was trying to take something out of her eyes as I went close to her to help, but she screamed and said, "Lysandros, no! It's glass. My tears become glass and every time, I become blind again. It repairs on its own after a while, but please don't touch it as you will cut your fingers. I don't want you touching me because what if by that, you too become a prisoner in this world? I don't know if it is Hell or purgatory or what, as I do not even remember committing any grave sins known to me. However, I am still here."

Linus walked in front of her and blew on her eyes. Ambers of gold light flew out of his mouth and landed on her eyes. Maharani opened her eyes and smiled. I watched Linus hug and kiss Maharani on her head. He wiped her tears as they now fell freely without freezing like glass.

I told everyone, "Maybe it's my sin, as traditional marriages say, 'till death do us apart.' We wanted our vows to be eternal, so we said, 'in this life and next, for eternity.' We knew somehow our love story would be short-lived, yet we wanted to be together forever. Yes, somehow, I had given up immortality for my beloved and I would give it up over and over again as I believe eternally, I am hers in life or after death. Not physically but through our love story, may we be immortal."

Geeta was again playing with her hands as Dirk too picked up her habit and was copying her. They were both making fists and I assumed it was because they wanted to fist out the demon physically as both were very emotionally invested in this love story.

I knew my love story was going to end soon, so I told Maharani, "I know wedding vows say till death do us apart, yet we said in our vows eternally. I know I have reincarnated, and you have not, so we are separated by a breath. Yet I have your memories and will wait out my life to be reborn for you with you in our next life or wherever you may be. I have all my love and my memories safely placed within my chest until then. I promise I will open the door of death or life to be with you. The only path I see is through innocent prayers which I will not stop reciting until we meet again."

My whole house full of people forgot to smile as everyone had tears falling from their eyes. Maybe we could combine our tears and create an ocean to keep Maharani within. Yet at every sound and noise, we all screamed, "The Grim Reaper? Is he here?"

Maharani then was praying loudly as she said, "Dear Grim Reaper, take me away as you please. Leave my beloved, his friends, and family members alone. Please leave the twin girls who carry my Lysandros's name and my Linus's blood alone. Let them always be safe. I take a vow to carry all the burdens and all the pain and sins of everyone, so they do not touch them."

Tears spilled from my eyes, and I asked them to stop pouring. Why did my eyes betray me like this? I tried to roll the tears back into my eyes with force as I tried to listen to my beloved.

She said to the Grim Reaper, "Please tell me, why is it? I never was reborn, yet my twin flame was! What did I do wrong? I just wanted to be with him eternally. Is falling in love a sin? Then, why does God allow not only mortals, but also spirits who roam around after death to feel and to love? Why did God create twin flames if they are not to be united? My heartbeats are frozen in time, yet my love for Lysandros will never cease."

The whole room felt like it was witnessing a heavy pour. The pouring was not from the skies but from the eyes of all the witnesses of a romance tragedy. It was then we heard a huge sigh come from the Grim Reaper's voice.

He was there like a fog. He was visible but invisible. He watched everyone from under his hooded cloak. We saw within the ocean, he was in his gondola, far away from the castle yet I felt like he was not far enough. His eyes or face were not visible.

He walked on his gondola, stood on top of the ocean waves, and said, "Your father murdered your beloved without any mercy. He even recited a spell to have your beloved's face. Even when all of these phenomena were occurring, your beloved recited to the Creator, 'Oh my God I don't know why this man's revenge has converted him into a monster, yet as I take my last breath, I forgive him, not so I forgive his sins but so I am free from all of his sins and my guilt of why he did this.'"

The Grim Reaper was staring at the castle and all its inhabitants. The whole situation felt like we were all in a fog and could see everything but were not capable of moving. We were all frozen in the mystical dark fog.

The Grim Reaper with a very stern voice said again, "You did not. As you were dying, you said, 'I want to live eternally only to hunt him down. I want revenge for all the wrong he has committed. Even if it takes thousands of years, I want revenge!' You see the difference? Your heart became infected with the evil person's darkness. You became like him. You were hungry for revenge. Yet Lysandros's heart never did. Even to his death, he repeated 'Forgive me for I forgive all.'"

I watched Maharani cry and shake her head as she agreed with him. She looked at him and signaled him to just take her as she was ready.

The Grim Reaper said, "Lysandros forgave and asked for forgiveness. Revenge and hatred are two of the deadliest sins. They infect not one but all lives throughout time. Forgiveness is divine. It removes all sins related to the predator. Divine is choosing to release and letting go of all unresolved hurt. Forgive all as you too seek forgiveness from all. Hatred is one of the deadliest sins that keeps you from moving on. Let go and learn to forgive."

The castle and the whole area were now covered within a blue fog. As the dark black fog was lifting, it was becoming blue, and everything was slowly fading. Maharani looked at me as I saw she was fading even more. I worried what if tomorrow at dawn my Maharani was no more. What if she became dust to dust? I would keep her memories alive within me if my heart kept beating as Maharani, my beloved twin flame, and I are separated by a heartbeat.

SEPARATED BY A HEARTBEAT

Lying in bed,
I hear
My warm
And hot body's
Heartbeats racing,
Longing to go somewhere.
Yet I watch
My beloved sweetheart
Stand and watch
Me sleeping,
As she stands
By the open doors
With her cold,
Freezing,
Transparent body,
Where her heart
Longs for me.
Her inner heart cries
Because of our memories.
She tried
To forget me
Yet could not.
Her tears had frozen,

Yet her feelings
Never froze.
Her longing
Never ceased.
Yet then I ask,
How is it
Her heart beats
No more
As we are
SEPARATED BY A HEARTBEAT?

Epilogue:

Submerged Ever After

"The Grim
Reaper's gondola
carries the dead
away, yet
prayer calls
from true
lovers are
answered, as they
are eternally submerged
ever after."

The day was a hot and sunny day. It was a very pleasant day. Not too sunny or too hot but perfect tropical weather. No teary clouds appeared in the skies as all the tears from the skies were placed within my eyes. The people were all going to church as it was Sunday.

Children looked forward to a day out at the beach. A lot of small island markets were set up for after church shoppers. Fresh seafood, root vegetables, tropical fruits, bread, and pies were being baked in open beach ovens made of clay. Church bells were ringing, calling everyone in. The island became a vacationer's paradise all over again.

I avoided churches these days. I worried what if God was angry with me for not being able to keep Maharani with me. Maybe it was all my fault. I prayed each day at home and by the ocean to be forgiven for falling in love with the Dead Queen. I reminded everyone that I fell in love with her when she was alive. I just never fell out of love even after she died, and I reincarnated with my memories.

Geeta and Dirk stayed on the island with me, as they fell in love and got married a month after Maharani disappeared. Linus and Alala too remained on the island and got to see their daughters who were three months old now. Their daughters were the love and life of everyone in our castle. They kept my heartbeats going as I loved them more than my misery. Mum and Aunt Grace came and gave Dirk and Geeta the children as I told my mother that's what Linus and his wife would want. Because of my mother and Aunt Grace's age, this was the right decision.

Our old, feared castle now had babies crying and laughing. The islanders were not afraid of the castle anymore as everyone believed the babies got rid of all the ghosts and goblins. The castle had undergone a minor renovation as we all wanted it to look original with only minor decorations.

I hung portraits of Maharani which I painted by hand from my memories in the library and the main parlor. The plaque under each of her portraits read, "THE MOST LOVING WIFE OF KING LYSANDROS THE SECOND." Because Maharani's mother was of Indian origin, she was known as not just the Queen and Her Majesty. She was known by an Indian title, Maharani, or the great queen in English.

I wanted to leave the island and forget all my memories of Maharani. I wanted to move on, but I couldn't. The fear of what if she returned suddenly, then how would she find me, kept me steadfast within the castle. I also managed to fall in love with the positive versions of the castle and not fear the horrific side of it. This castle was the only place in this entire world where I knew Maharani once lived. So, how could I separate myself from here?

I kept hearing her words, "I give up everything only for you to live and be happy. Please keep me alive through your soul. For if you breathe, how can I not? For if you live, how can I not? When you see blooming flowers on the wall, remember me. Each morning as the birds sing their sweet songs, know I too am singing with them only for you."

Memories of my beloved were so powerful that I found it easy to move on. Who said one can't love in separation? Who said one can't dream when awake, and one can't feel the beloved when they are physically not here?

I remembered my beloved's words again as she had said, "Watch the night stars and never give up hope on us my beloved. I will blink from Heavens above like a star only to guide you. Forever I will be in your soul as your twin flame, through my love for you and your love for me. Breathe my beloved and know you must live and breathe for both of us for I will be there through your breath. You now breathe for both of our souls."

Alala flew over the skies as I saw a lightning bolt fly above me. She was giving her daughters a ride above the ocean. It felt kind of good to know Linus and Alala could still be with their children. They loved Geeta and Dirk for giving the babies a normal mortal life. These bundles of joys had two sets of parents, and I was their godfather as I would hold them in my empty chest for eternity.

Geeta came out and lovingly said, "Alala, may I have my daughters back? It's their nap time and this Aunty of theirs can't take a nap without them. They know they have a Mama and Papa who will come and go, but this Aunty will never let them be alone."

Geeta gave me tea with cream, sugar, and a fresh cinnamon stick on top of it. She also made fresh buttermilk biscuits and left me some to eat as I finished my novel. I had come to this island months ago to write a novel amongst other things. Never did I know I would be writing my own love story filled with so many miracles. My publisher called this book a gothic romance fiction. How would they know this was based on truth, not just my imagination?

I watched the ocean from my veranda as I sipped my tea. I believed the ocean waves spoke to me as she knew within her soul were hidden the secrets of my love story. The ocean seemed upset and angry as the waves became higher and higher.

Maybe the ocean was lonely and was trying to kiss its soulmate on land. I watched how they touched then separated as the waves calmed down. The waves waited and the Earth knew soon they would meet again. Its beloved would come back as the waves got higher. I knew my beloved walked into the land of the dead and in life and death, there was no return.

Geeta ran back outside and stood behind me as she said, "The girls are napping, and Dirk is back. He said Aunt Valery and Aunt Grace are doing well back home in Tasmania. They're still upset and cry a lot but said they know their time will come soon for them to unite with Linus and Alala. So, they want to live with love, honor, and dignity until then. You know, I love your mother and Aunt Grace's way of seeing the world. I want to take so much of their teachings within my soul to teach the girls."

Geeta was talking nonstop. I didn't even realize when Dirk was back standing behind me.

He cleared his voice and said, "You won't even ask how my trip was? Am I okay? Or ahh so good to have you back home. Missed you so much. Come on Lysandros, buddy, please try to live life for her even without her. It's not easy, but that's the message of life. Live for her even without her."

I only smiled, as suddenly the wind picked up. I imagined the wind was my beloved blowing kisses, telling me to be happy for her. I felt like staying quiet and not saying anything. Even talking bothered me. I hadn't shaved for a while and had a small beard which made me look as depressing on the outside as I felt on the inside. My khaki pants and khaki shirt blew in the wind as I enjoyed the ocean breeze so much. I always imagined the morning breeze to be my beloved's kisses as it came and touched me in the morning saying, "Good morning." The night breeze told me, "Good night, until we meet again."

Alala lifted her wings in front of me as she said, "Lysandros, everyone is worried if you are thinking of committing suicide. We're all worried, the dead and the living. No, I don't know anything about Maharani, or where she is. I don't know if she is in purgatory, or in Heaven, or in the canal of rebirth. I tried to find out but for the thousandth time, I don't know. If I did, then you would be the first to know."

Geeta was sitting and standing as she was nervous and could not decide if she should sit or stand. I got to know this woman so much better in the last few months. It felt strange how I ever lasted without her. She called me her brother as I accepted both Geeta and Alala as my sisters.

I broke out in a laughing fit for some strange reason as I told both my sisters, "No, I won't commit any sins. Not in this life or in any, at least not to my knowledge. I won't stop praying or believing we will unite in this life or in another. I will wait for eternity with my mortal soul to have not one but all my lives with her. Love doesn't die with the body as love is eternal and so is my love for my beloved."

The skies suddenly went dark, and the winds picked up. Not again, I thought. I couldn't go through this all over again. Somehow something was happening. Alala and Geeta ran trying to take things into the house as we assumed it had to be a normal Earthly storm.

I shouted and told Dirk over the high winds, "Take the babies and go to the cellar. Keep them there where I was in prison. They will be safe there. Go now both of you. Geeta and Dirk, go run! You will have my protection and the protection of my forefathers in there."

Dirk and Geeta ran with the two bundles of joy. They never questioned as all we cared for at this time was to keep the babies safe. Linus and Alala were with me as we watched the ocean rise. There was a gondola coming toward the castle. It was brown and gold. In the gondola, we could all clearly see was a person covered in black. It was the Grim Reaper himself and his boat.

Alala said, "What's going on? Why is he here? Who will he take now? Oh my God, he is here to take me and Linus to purgatory or maybe directly to Heavens above as we were murdered by a demon. I wanted some time with my girls, but it's okay. We are ready, right Linus? Did you get to kiss the babies goodbye? I made it a habit to kiss them every time I leave because I don't know if that would be the last time we could see them."

Linus stood in front of me and was holding on to me. He knew he was immortal as was his wife, so he worried if the Grim Reaper came for me. I laughed as I saw the winds increased. Trees were blowing away in all different directions. Garden furniture pieces were going in all different directions, yet we didn't move from our places.

Dirk and Geeta came and joined us as he said, "The girls are with the babysitter. We want to be with you if the Grim Reaper comes to take you. I will ask him how he is stronger than our combined prayers. Does he not fear his own Creator? Prayers are sent to the Creator of everyone, of him and us. So, why is it we should fear him, and he does not fear our prayers?"

I watched my friends and knew I too loved them and would do the same. Yet I wondered if it was my time, then maybe I would unite with Maharani again in the next life sooner rather than later. I didn't say my thoughts out loud as that would immensely hurt my friends. So, I remained quiet.

When the winds caught up with heavy pouring rain, it was bone-chilling cold. It wasn't normal for this region, but I never said anything about the weather these days as climate change was another issue I knew was happening and was not the effects of any paranormal activities. Maybe an islander was taking a boat ride in the stormy weather.

It was like the boat was taking forever to come within our clear viewing distance. The boat came closer and closer slowly. We saw there were two people on board. One was wearing all black and had his head covered. The other one was small and wore white. She had her hair loose blowing in the wind. I realized who it was but wondered how and why. I said nothing out loud but started to run toward the water.

I climbed down the huge boulders and jumped into the ocean. Dirk jumped over with me as he tried to pull me back to shore where the boat docked. Dirk was a lifeguard as well as my ship's captain.

He said, "Stupid! You don't know how to swim, remember? Why would you jump over when he is coming to shore? Like we all said, we won't let you die in this life this early, and even if the Grim Reaper comes, he will have to go against our prayers directly recited to God the Omnipotent."

The boat docked. A very tall maybe eight-foot-tall man dressed in a black cloak stepped off the boat. His eyes were covered by his hood.

He walked closer to us and said with a very poised voice, "I the Grim Reaper must say, even I cannot take away a soul who is protected and loved by his twin flame so much. Yes, normally I come to take people through the door of death. Yet by God's commands, I have come for the first time to say, I am not taking a life but bringing back someone dead who shall have one life to live with her beloved as a living and breathing woman. Then, they can again reincarnate together. It is God the Creator's wish and the prayers of innocent souls which have been answered. I pray may you two be together not just in this life but all lives to come, be together. Yes, I the creation too fear and love my God, my Creator, and I do as He wishes."

The darkness evaporated as we were all now standing under a bright sunny sky. The sun's rays were warming up the world as my friends and I knew we were witnessing the first glimpse of a new dawn. This miracle, from the beyond, was like how dawn breaks out every morning to greet the world back into light after a dark night's journey through darkness. Maharani walked toward me as I went and held her in my arms. To hold her like this was for me to have a clear breath in years. It was as if for all this time, I was running a marathon while holding on to my breath.

Maharani said, "From soul to soul, my husband, I have said when the path drifts us apart, or the road sets us apart, or life and death keeps us apart, love me from soul to soul, and pray our love story reaches God the Omnipotent. Love and twin flames shall unite through answered prayers in life or in death. Who says prayers are not accepted or answered? They are. We must be patient and wait because at times it may take over a thousand years."

The day was filled with love and joy, as my beloved held the twins in her arms. She cried and kissed them both, holding them in her chest. The babies opened their eyes and smiled at her.

She was jumping in joy as she said, "They are my blood! They come from my Linus. Dear God, thank you! I am blessed now I can be a part of their life. Forever, I promise I will protect them within the power of my love."

The ocean waves became so loud that I wondered if they too were rejoicing or maybe they knew something I did not. Yet I learned in this life, I would take each day as a miracle. Without any hesitation, or anyone's permission or disapproval, I held my beloved within my chest and kissed her on her lips. Frightened to be separated from her, I just wanted to hold her in my chest for eternity.

I told my beloved, "Let our love story be spoken from soul to soul. True lovers and true love stories don't ever die. Even though we have one life to live, you don't need to be immortal as it's the love story that is immortal. From this day forward for love and from love, let the world sing in union, the gondola returns as the Dead Queen rises."

Forty days and forty nights after the return of Maharani, the Dead Queen's Island was no more as it went under the ocean. We lived within the castle and the island as if nothing had happened. Our existence continued under the ocean. Dirk, Geeta, Linus, Alala, Maharani, the twin girls, and I all lived under the ocean.

We realized our island didn't exist anymore. We all chose to be with our beloved family members under the ocean. We didn't know what happened to our family members above the ocean, but we were at peace knowing each day under the ocean was like a hundred Earth years.

Linus came to me and said, "I wonder if the world even remembers there once upon a time was an island called the Dead Queen's Island. The whole island still existed. Those who never left still lived on the island just like they lived before. They didn't realize they were living not above

Earth but under the ocean. My wife and I accepted you all as our family, so I guess we got another chance to be buried with you all in a life together under the ocean."

I realized our island was not in any map or anyone's memories anymore. No one ever recorded our names or our stories. Our castle, church, and marketplace, all were buried under the water with all our love stories. We were all buried under the ocean when we accepted the miracle. The gondola and the Dead Queen returned, and we with our whole island were submerged ever after.

The End.

Or the beginning of a love story that began above the Earth and now is still being written under the ocean.

SUBMERGED EVER AFTER

Separated
By a breath,
Yet connected through
Each breath.
How it is
My heart beats
When your heart beats
No more?
From my mind,
Body,
And soul,
I call upon you.
Under the starless skies,
Beneath the deep ocean,
Above the cold Earth,
I see everyone
Except you.
So tonight,
I call you
From my soul
To yours.
Through the bond
Of twin flames,

SUBMERGED EVER AFTER

I call you.
As I open my chest,
I ask,
Seek,
And call
The Creator
For a miracle
To be with you
Within the land
Of the dead
Or for you
To be with me
Within the land
Of the living.
Oh,
My beloved,
Hold me
As I hold you tenderly
And lovingly
Within my chest.
Today,
As I open my eyes,
I see my darling
Loves me too.

My sweetheart,
For the Dead Queen who rose,
Our entire island
For love,
With love,
And believing in only true love,
SUBMERGED EVER AFTER.

Message From The Author

"I love you
in life and in
death, yet I can't
control my last
heartbeats as
I ask you to
keep me
with love,
submerged
within you."

In each one of my books, I leave you with a message, a special note, my own reason for writing the book. Here I've written about fear, judgment, and love. A person's personal fear, personal judgment, and personal attachment by love can conclude their perception perceived through their evaluation of any assumed circumstances.

These personal perceptions clouded by fear can make or break a person's life. When one person's judgment influences a group, a society, or a country, that's when even the innocent becomes the guilty as perceived through the minds of the perceivers. It's like everyone fears the dead, not the living. Yet I ask you, why? The dead can't harm you, but the living and breathing can. Judgments given because you feel like that's the right thing is wrong if you don't have the facts. Falling in love but too scared to fight for your love as he or she might be fighting death is wrong. I believe love even for a day is worth the day, if your heart feels like it is your love story.

Through this book, I want you all to not fear the dead, not judge the others, but do fall in love when your heart calls for it. Write your love story through the days of your life. Don't become the prey or the victim and lose it all as we all only have one life to live. Love is immortal even though humans are not. Mortals become immortal as they enter the gondolas of immortal love stories.

Therefore, all humans who have fallen in love become immortal through their love stories. The love story can be between a mother and her children, between a father and his children, between siblings, between friends, and between twin souls. True love is an unconditional, divine, and timeless gift.

In each one of my books, I leave you with a very personal message. My own perception prompted me to give you a book where my message is fall in love even if this love is for a short period of time. Don't let the most fearsome journey called death prevent you from falling in love. Don't fear death or the dead, as the person you fear today was standing by you yesterday when he or she was breathing. Hold on to the most powerful blessing called the miracle of love to defeat all your fear. Like a shield, hold it near your heart as you will hear the musical drumbeats on it, which will say, "I love you for eternity."

Love is victorious. Love is fearless. Love floods your eyes with tears to wipe away all the thorns. Love is eternal when the lovers dance through life and death with one another, for one another. From this book, carry within your soul the magical elixir of love. Spread it all over yourself and all others through the journey of your life.

I believe love can be cherished even when the lovers are apart. Love is eternal even when the lovers are separated through a breath. Love is the magical elixir which you don't sip yourself but want your beloved to sip and be immortal for you. Now try to say the magical words, "I love you through life and even after death." This will be your eternal vow that will bind you to your twin flame eternally.

I know in this world we have so many burdens to carry over the bridge of life. Yet even for a short period of time, I want you to take a break. Forget all your troubles and take a vacation through this magical island. Here you will see everyone fears her, everyone gossips about her, everyone calls her names. Yet why don't you the reader open your eyes like Lysandros Ealdwine and defend her honor?

Spread the eternal message of true love and its immortal existence throughout the world through all libraries. Go out there and tell the world not to judge everyone before they too have read the whole story. Teach everyone not to fear the dead because they had to take a one-way ticket out of this world within the gondola of the Grim Reaper.

I was once shocked as my close friends refused to buy a house because they found out the previous owner had taken his last breath in the house. His wife and children were selling the house and didn't share the reason for selling. They didn't fear the undisclosed truth but the dead person. What if he still walks as a ghost in the house?

I told my friends, then fear the world for the forefathers of this world are dead. It's a sad story when a loving house remains on the market today because the previous owners had died inside of it. Yet the previous owners wanted to take their last breath in their loving home knowing it was where they found peace.

My answer to all of you the petrified is don't fear the dead. Maybe try to see why they are not in peace if they are still roaming around. In this book, there is a woman who is feared, whose life story too is forgotten and fearsome. No one remembers why she never left, but she is believed to be the dark Dead Queen from a thousand years ago. Research the dead and try to give them some dignity for living through this unjust world. We the living must try to live with the same dignity. Don't fear, don't judge, and don't throw stones at true love and lovers.

As I began to write this immortal love story, I asked what is love through my eyes? If I knew the person I love only had a few days left on this Earth, would I still marry him? I answered my own question.

Love is the feeling of oneness, recognition of belonging, and recognition of another soul. Love is not defined by lust or power, but through unconditional, selfless, and divine connection of the mind, the body, and the soul. Even if you are loved or can love for a day, love becomes immortal through the love story of the two. I believe love is immortal, so falling in love makes the lovers immortal through their love story.

Can the dead return? What if one twin flame is living and the other one is dead? I have woven a novel where the bridge of life and death is overcome through memories, reincarnation, and immortal love stories. Believe in the miracles of life. If the Grim Reaper can take a person from the world of the living to the world of the dead, then why can't he bring them back from the world of the dead to the world of the living? Well in my world of fiction, it is possible as I believe in miracles of the pen.

You too should believe in your dreams and believe in your twin flame and believe in the prayers of the twin flames. So, now I want you all to go ahead and dream a little. Make your dreams come true through the bridge of faith and miracles. Just know with faith, everything is possible. Life is a short journey. Live with and for love. For even when the journey of life ends, true love stories do not end as the readers yesterday, today, and tomorrow will keep reading the love stories, making them immortal.

Now hold my hands and let's again take a trip to a faraway island not known or visited by many. There a lonely soul waits for her incomplete love story to be completed in happily ever after. The only thing that has kept her and her twin flame apart is just one single heartbeat. Let all the hearts that beat today on Earth remember her love story and keep it eternal.

I call this book *Submerged Ever After*, as I submerge my mind, my body, and my soul to true love and ever after stories. Now go ahead and read the book again. Share the book with your friends and read along with them. Submerge yourselves within true love and know love is eternal, love is immortal, and love stories are happily ever after in separation, in union, in life, or in death.

Happy reading everyone!

SUBMERGED WITHIN YOU

My love for you is
Eternal.
My love story with you is
Infinite.
My call for you is
Divine.
My past with you is
Passionate.
My present with you is
Emotional.
My future with you is
Devotional.
My universe is
SUBMERGED WITHIN YOU.

Dwellers Within Submerged Ever After

Lysandros Ealdwine	Famous author, owner of the Dead Queen's Island and Dead Queen's Castle, son of Valery Ealdwine, and twin flame and husband of Maharani Aarna.
Maharani Aarna	Dead Queen, twin flame and wife of Lysandros Ealdwine.
Dr. Linus Didáskalos	Lysandros's childhood friend, Doctor of Parapsychology, descendant of Lysandros and Maharani Aarna, son of Grace Didáskalos, twin flame and husband of Alala Didáskalos.
Alala Didáskalos	Twin flame and wife of Linus Didáskalos.
Captain Dirk van Schipper	Childhood friend of Lysandros Ealdwine, lifeguard and ship captain for Lysandros Ealdwine, twin flame and husband of Dr. Geeta Shrivastava.
Dr. Geeta Shrivastava	Doctor for Ealdwine Family and Group business, twin flame and wife of Captain Dirk van Schipper

King Villainous	Previous owner of the Dead Queen's Castle, father of Maharani Aarna.
Valery Ealdwine	Mother of Lysandros Ealdwine, Aunt of Dr. Linus Didáskalos.
Grace Didáskalos	Mother of Linus Didáskalos, Aunt of Lysandros Ealdwine.
Ms. Baker	Alala Didáskalos's house helper.
Ashok Mitra	Ealdwine Family and Group business manager
Captain Anthony	Ship captain for Lysandros Ealdwine.
Divya	Sister of Maharani Aarna.
Vidya	Sister of Maharani Aarna.

Glossary

Get acquainted with some terms and places that were used in this book.

Anjali Mudra Sanskrit term meaning sign of salutation, refers to positioning two hands together with palms touching in a prayer pose

Australia Largest country in Oceania and sixth-largest country in the world

Dingo Wild dogs in Australia

Grim Reaper Cloaked figure that represents death

India Country in South Asia, amongst the most populated countries in the world

Indian Ocean Third-largest ocean in the world between Asia, Africa, Australia, and Antarctica

Maharani Sanskrit term meaning great queen, also refers to the wife or widow of a king

Naarden City in the Netherlands, home of the Kasteel Vrederic book series

Pacific Ocean	Largest ocean in the world between Asia, Australia, North America, South America, and Antarctica
Parapsychology	Study of psychic and paranormal activities
Purgatory	Catholic concept of stage before entering Heaven where soul undergoes cleansing and purification
South East Cape	Southern most edge of Australia and the Australian state of Tasmania
Tasmania	Southernmost island-state of Australia that includes over 1,000 smaller islands
Tasmanian Devil	Nocturnal carnivorous marsupial in Tasmania known for their screeching at night
The Netherlands	Country in Northwestern Europe

About The Author

"Meet Ann Marie Ruby from Nashville, Tennessee. This is her story."

Ann Marie Ruby was born into a diplomatic family for which she had the privilege of traveling the world. This upbringing made the whole world her one family. She never saw a country as a foreign country yet as a neighbor who was there for her as she would be there for them. After all, isn't that what families do for one another?

Ann Marie became an author as she started to place her chosen words into the pages of her diaries. She knew she must collect all her thoughts and produce them into different diaries. Each diary became her different books.

Ann Marie's life goal is not to just write something but only what she believes in. So all her thoughts and words remained within the pages of her diaries until she realized it was time she must share them with you. Otherwise, she felt selfish and knew that was not her characteristic as she lives for everyone, not just for herself.

INTERNATIONAL #1 BESTSELLING AUTHOR:

Ann Marie became an international number-one bestselling author of thirty books. Alongside being a full-time author. She loves to write articles on her website where she can have a better connection with all of you. Ann Marie, a dream psychic, became a blogger and a humanitarian only because she believes in you and herself as a complete, honest, and open family.

PERSONAL:

Ann Marie is an American who grew up in Brisbane, Australia. She has resided all across the United States and is currently living in Nashville, Tennessee. In her spare time when she is not writing books, she loves to meditate, pray, listen to music, cook, and write blog posts.

BESTSELLING:

Ann Marie's books have placed her on top 100 bestselling charts in various countries including the Netherlands, United States, United Kingdom, Canada, and Germany. In 2020, she became a household name as her books began to consistently rank #1 on multiple bestselling charts. *The Netherlands: Land Of My Dreams* and *Everblooming: Through The Twelve Provinces Of The Netherlands*, both became overnight number-one bestsellers in the United States.

In 2020, *The Netherlands: Land Of My Dreams* also became a bestseller in the Netherlands and Canada, consistently becoming #1 on various lists and one of the top selling books on Amazon NL. *Everblooming: Through The Twelve Provinces Of The Netherlands* became #37 on the Netherlands top 100 bestselling Amazon books chart which includes all books from all genres. Ann Marie's other books have also made various top 100 bestselling lists and received multiple accolades including *Eternal Truth: The Tunnel Of Light* which was named as one of eight thought-provoking books by women.

ROMANCE FICTION:

Ann Marie's *Kasteel Vrederic* series was written in a diary fashion. She has always kept a diary herself, so she thought her characters too could keep a diary. All of their diaries became individual books yet collectively, they are a part of a family, the Kasteel Vrederic family.

OTHER BOOKS:

All of Ann Marie's nonfiction and fiction books are available globally. You can take a look at the titles at the end of this book.

THE NETHERLANDS:

Ann Marie revealed why many of her books revolve around the Netherlands, sharing that as a dream psychic, she had seen the historical past of a country in her dreams and was later able to place a name to the country. This is described in detail in *Spiritual Lighthouse: The Dream Diaries Of Ann Marie Ruby* and *The Netherlands: Land Of My Dreams* where she also wrote about her plans to eventually move to the Netherlands.

Ann Marie has received letters on behalf of His Majesty King Willem-Alexander and Her Majesty Queen Máxima of the Netherlands after they received her books *The Netherlands: Land Of My Dreams* and *Everblooming: Through The Twelve Provinces Of The Netherlands.* Additionally, Ann Marie has received letters on behalf of His Excellency Mark Rutte, the Prime Minister of the Netherlands for her books.

WRITING:

Ann Marie also is acclaimed globally as one of the top voices in the spiritual space, however, she is recognized for her writing abilities published across many genres namely spirituality, lifestyle, inspirational quotations, poetry, fiction, romance, history, travel, social awareness, and more. Her writing style is hailed by critics and readers alike as making readers feel as though they have made a friend.

FOLLOW THE AUTHOR:

Now as you have found her book, why don't you and Ann Marie become friends? Join her and become a part of her global family. Ann Marie shall always give you books which you will read and then find yourself as a part of her book family.

For more information about Ann Marie Ruby, any one of her books, or to read her blog posts and articles, subscribe to her website, www.annmarieruby.com.

Follow Ann Marie Ruby on Twitter, Facebook, Instagram, Threads, and Pinterest:

@TheAnnMarieRuby

BOOKS BY THE AUTHOR

INSPIRATIONAL QUOTATIONS:

1. *Spiritual Travelers: Life's Journey From The Past To The Present For The Future*
2. *Spiritual Messages: From A Bottle*
3. *Spiritual Journey: Life's Eternal Blessings*
4. *Spiritual Inspirations: Sacred Words Of Wisdom*
5. *Spiritual Ark: The Enchanted Journey Of Timeless Quotations*

SPIRITUAL SONGS SERIES:

1. *Spiritual Songs: Letters From My Chest*
2. *Spiritual Songs II: Blessings From A Sacred Soul*
3. *Spiritual Songs III: The Rising Lotus*
4. *Spiritual Songs IV: Dusk Through Dawn*
5. *Spiritual Songs V: Dawn Through Dusk*

KASTEEL VREDERIC SERIES:

1. *Eternally Beloved: I Shall Never Let You Go*
2. *Evermore Beloved: I Shall Never Let You Go*
3. *Be My Destiny: Vows From The Beyond*
4. *Heart Beats Your Name: Vows From The Beyond*
5. *Entranced Beloved: I Shall Never Let You Go*
6. *Forbidden Daughter Of Kasteel Vrederic: Vows From The Beyond*
7. *The Immortality Serum: Vows From The Beyond*
8. *Woman In The Mirror: Vows From The Beyond*

Upcoming – *Bride Of The Immortal: Vows From The Beyond*

RELATED TO THE *KASTEEL VREDERIC* SERIES:

1. *Shattered Wings: Diary Of A Child Bride*

2. *The Bride, The Groom, And The Ghost*
3. *The Haunting Of MacNider Hospital*
4. *Submerged Ever After*
5. *Enchanted Tales: A Kasteel Vrederic Storybook For Children*

Upcoming – *Brother Bear And The Four Investigators: A Kasteel Vrederic Storybook For Children*

NONFICTION:

1. *Spiritual Lighthouse: The Dream Diaries Of Ann Marie Ruby*
2. *The World Hate Crisis: Through The Eyes Of A Dream Psychic*
3. *Eternal Truth: The Tunnel Of Light*

TRAVEL:

1. *The Netherlands: Land Of My Dreams*
2. *Everblooming: Through The Twelve Provinces Of The Netherlands*

POETRY:

1. *Love Letters: The Timeless Treasure*
2. *Melodies Of Humanity: The Golden Keys*

www.ingramcontent.com/pod-product-compliance
Lightning Source LLC
LaVergne TN
LVHW090550110826
845146LV00001B/95

* 9 7 9 8 9 9 5 0 5 9 5 0 9 *